Born Twice

Born Twice

by

GIUSEPPE PONTIGGIA

*Translated from the Italian
by Oonagh Stransky*

Alfred A. Knopf   New York   2002

THIS IS A BORZOI BOOK
PUBLISHED BY ALFRED A. KNOPF

Translation copyright © 2002 by Alfred A. Knopf,
a division of Random House, Inc.

www.aaknopf.com

Originally published in Italy as *Nati Due Volte* by
Arnoldo Mondadori S.p.A., Milan, in 2000.
Copyright © 2000 by Arnoldo Mondadori, S.p.A., Milan.

Library of Congress Cataloging-in-Publication Data
Pontiggia, Giuseppe, 1934–
[Nati due volte. English]
Born twice / by Giuseppe Pontiggia ; translated from the Italian by
Oonagh Stransky.—
1. American ed.
p.   cm.
ISBN 0-375-41310-3
I. Stransky, Oonagh.   II. Title.

PQ4876.O53 N3713 2002
853'.914—dc21   2002016259

Manufactured in the United States of America
First American Edition

For the disabled
who struggle not to be normal
but to be themselves

CONTENTS

CONTENTS

Born Twice

Escalators

The escalators leading to the third floor rise steeply between a set of descending ones, the steps above us disappear into the overhead lights, and a dense crowd circulates slowly below on the receding walkways.

"Do you like it?" I lean forward and ask, my face close to his ear.

"Yes," he replies, without looking back.

Gripping the rubber handrail with his left hand, he lets his body lean back into my arms, which he can feel are open behind him. I shift my weight forward to support his. When we reach the top, where the metal steps recede into a dark fissure, he loses his balance and stumbles forward.

"Don't worry, I've got you!" I say, reaching out for him.

He doesn't fall. He positions himself on the carpet just beyond the landing, his legs and feet stiff with tension. He takes a few steps. I look around and wipe my brow with my hand. A woman is staring at us coldly. She's standing next to a yellow beach umbrella that has been planted in a square of sand meant to simulate a beach scene. I stare back at her. I'm tired of people staring. But then she gasps, her hand goes to her mouth, and I hear a heavy thud. It's Paolo. He's fallen on his side. He rolled over onto his back, the way they taught him to do at school, but too late. His face is twisted in pain, the palms of his hands flat on the floor.

"Are you hurt?" I whisper, crouching down beside him.

He shakes his head. I position his feet against mine and pull him up. A small crowd of curious and alarmed onlookers has formed. They retreat to let us by.

"Everything's fine," I say.

I help him along for a few steps.

"Do you feel better now?"

"Yes."

I point out a nearby stand covered with palm fronds. It's surrounded by small tropical plants and set against a blue cardboard backdrop.

"Do you feel like getting something to drink?"

"Yes."

We sit down on benches at a rustic wooden table. A giant plastic shark next to us displays an array of fishing gear in its jaws. I look at its sharp, crooked teeth. I'm exhausted and unhappy.

"Do you want a Coke?" I ask.

"Yes."

I hold his glass for him while he drinks from it. Then we get up to leave.

"Go slowly now. Pay attention," I say gently.

I watch him walk off, reeling like a drunken sailor. No, like a spastic.

Suddenly he turns and says in that labored way of his, "If you're embarrassed you don't have to walk next to me. I'll be all right."

Coming into the World

I'm at school when he's about to be born. I've already started teaching my class. The ordinarily grumpy custodian comes into the room with a wide smile on her face. She walks over to the lectern and whispers in my ear.

"Professore, your wife is at the hospital. Her mother called. She asked me to tell you. She said there's no hurry."

I look at the class calmly.

"Her water broke," she adds.

I nod dispassionately. What does that mean? How does water break? Maybe it's the placenta. I visualize torn membranes and dripping fluids.

"You can cancel class if you want," she suggests.

"No, I'll keep going."

What an idiot. You want to show everyone, yourself above all, just how strong you are. How courageous when faced with danger. Only you're not the one who's in danger. I didn't think about that then. How calm we are when faced with dangers that are not our own.

Above all, show no emotion. Millennia of male-dominated

education encapsulated in a millisecond. I look at the class. They must have guessed by now. A girl in the front row overheard a few words the custodian said and turned to tell a friend. I smile. Everything's under control.

"Let's go on with the lesson," I say.

"Breech birth," the doctor says in the hospital corridor, without looking at me. Fat, beady-eyed, and out of breath, he looks like a large trapped mouse.

"Meaning?"

"Meaning he's breech." He looks up to make sure I don't understand.

"What complications are there, exactly?"

"It's hard to say. The greatest danger is anoxia."

"You mean the baby won't be able to breathe?"

"Something like that," he concedes, annoyed. "His heartbeat is regular; there's no need to intervene yet."

"What do you mean by intervene?"

"Cesarean section. But your gynecologist doesn't want to. He's against them."

Against them? I can see his face in front of me, larger than life— his thinning white hair, an air of fatigue and ruin about him.

"We'd like to avoid a cesarean. Doctors perform them these days at the drop of a hat."

I listened with an intent expression on my face, but all the while I was thinking not about Franca but of the woman I had met again after so many years, the woman I would be seeing in only a few hours, even as I asked, "Is the baby in any danger?"

"Naturally," he replied. "How did Leopardi put it? 'A man

comes struggling into the world; / His birth is in the shadow of death.' But let's wait on the cesarean. Trust me."

He looked at me compassionately, with that mask of wisdom that some people acquire when they age but which is actually the final, definitive, and eternal stamp of stupidity. I had expressed my doubts about him, once, to my wife. We were on the escalators at the time.

"Are you sure he's a good gynecologist?" I had asked.

"He's the best," she had replied.

He's coming toward me with small hurried steps, rocking from side to side like a penguin.

"Don't worry," he says, which is the best way to make someone do precisely that. "You've got to be patient."

"But why isn't he born yet?"

"He's a big baby," he says with a sigh. "He doesn't want to come into the world." Then, with a wink and a smile, he adds, "Maybe he has a point."

I want to grab him by the shoulders and shake the hell out of him, but I can't bring myself to be hostile to the one person I suddenly perceive as my most feared enemy.

"Oh, thank goodness you're here, Dr. Merini!" my mother-in-law exclaims, rushing up to greet him, taking both his hands in hers. "Everything will be all right, won't it, Doctor?"

"But of course, Signora! It's just more complicated than usual. Let's give nature a chance."

"Just what I needed to hear!" she says, clasping his hands in hers. She's elegant, melodramatic, and arrogant. Always on the verge of a breakdown. Always seeking out anxieties to flaunt and fears to have quelled. "So long as nothing happens to my little girl!"

"Or to the baby," my own mother adds coldly, joining the group. She has been following the conversation from her post by the window, glancing over occasionally to remind us of her presence. Her face has assumed the stony gaze that used to frighten me as a child. "Let's not forget he's the one being born."

"Well, hello! I didn't know you were here!" my mother-in-law says, addressing her in the tone she reserves for unwelcome guests. "The baby, of course! Both of them, obviously!"

"You're the ones who ruled out a cesarean, after all," my mother says.

My mother-in-law turns sharply toward her. "What on earth are you saying? We didn't rule out anything. We'd just like to avoid an operation, if possible. And who is this *you*, anyway?"

"You and your daughter, with your theories on natural childbirth," my mother replies. Then she points at me. "Him too. It might look like he's listening, but who really knows what's going on in that head of his?"

"Why do you always have to be so sinister?" I ask, trying to hurt her.

I succeed. The insult seems to have hit home. She goes back to the window in a state of furious isolation. She was an amateur actress in her youth and has never forgotten it. Neither have I.

I remember isolated events, like movie stills, that I can't quite piece together.

The nun, walking out of the birthing room at the end of the corridor, passing me by, pretending not to see me. I catch up with her.

"What's going on in there?"

"Ask your doctor," she says.

Dr. Merini, ever more bewildered, saying, "I never thought

it would come to this." Seeing an idiot in distress is far more disturbing than seeing a blissful one.

"What do you mean you *never thought*?" I ask, finally grabbing him by the shoulders and shaking him, doing what I ought to have done twelve hours ago. Twelve whole hours have gone by and there's been no delivery, just excruciating agony. "What the hell is going on in there?"

"We're going to use forceps," he announces, extricating himself from my grasp.

"Why not a cesarean?"

"It's too late. The baby is already crowning."

Me, making my way to the hospital chapel through a haze of colored lights, kneeling down to pray, feeling like an actor reluctantly playing his part. What am I doing here? This is not my role.

But it is. The comedy is over; the tragedy is about to begin. You've been through tough times before and now you're finally being called to account. You knew it would come to this. Be strong, you're dealing with God. Don't see her for a month. No, that's too long: three weeks. You shut your eyes. It's not only the doctors' fault, it's your fault too. What on earth could you have been thinking? Never see her again. No, that's not what's being asked of you. Anyway, you'd be unhappy and that would just make things worse for everyone.

You hear a silent voice in your head. Yes. It's as if someone's head were nodding. Yes, you don't deserve it, but this is how it is. You cross yourself and murmur your thanks.

I can't remember now who mentioned that the baby didn't cry right away. What does that mean? Is it serious? Yes, very serious. He was cyanotic. I remember one word: *catatonic*. The surgeon said it on his way out. The only question you want to ask is the one they don't want to hear: What are the consequences? It's too early to tell. Maybe nothing. Take care of your wife.

She's lying in bed, staring out the window, pale, exhausted, troubled, and silent. Drops of rain slither down the glass. I take her limp hand in mine.

"You were amazing."

She shakes her head.

"Don't worry, everything will be all right."

She doesn't reply.

She tries to speak but her voice is hoarse. I lean down. My cheek brushes against her cold damp forehead.

"Have you seen the baby?" she asks.

"No."

"Go see him."

Whoever mentioned the joys of childbirth?

I'll never forget that tiny purple face. I'll never forget that fixed half-smile or his cone-shaped head. The image of a Mesopotamian divinity comes to mind. He's frightening and homely at the same time. The nurse approaches with him in her arms.

"We're going to place him in the incubator now," she says.

"But his head—"

"Oh, that's nothing," she replies, leaning over the bed to show him to his mother.

Behind Glass

We walk through the room as if at an aquarium, observing the newborns in their sealed glass parallelepipeds. There's a magnifying glass built into the top of his, a tiny porthole onto his small naked body. Through it I see his genitalia, enlarged. His left foot twitches as if an invisible electrical shock were pulsing through him at regular intervals. It was stronger before, the doctor with me says, but he's under sedation now.

His small tense fingers extend and contract convulsively, like a fan that opens slowly and then snaps shut.

"Is he epileptic?" I ask, with surreal calmness.

We behave this way with doctors in order to gain their confidence; they know it as well as we do. By deceiving each other, no one ever has to say the truth.

"We're still waiting for the results of the encephalogram," he says professionally.

Overhearing

The choked-up voice talking on the pay phone belongs to my father-in-law. He doesn't know I can hear him. He's standing next to a plate-glass window in one of the corridors at the hospital, talking to his son, Marco.

"Do you understand what I'm saying? He might even be retarded."

He's furious; his eyes are glaring with anger. I feel like pushing him through the glass, but somehow I find the afflicted expression on his face reassuring. He's exaggerating, I tell myself, like he always does. He magnifies danger, making everything seem much worse than it really is, so as better to accept an attenuated version. The thought of physical disability causes him enormous grief. He's the athletic one in the family, a believer in preventive medicine, a proponent of healthy living. He'll never succumb to old age.

"Don't ask me any more questions. We don't know—they don't tell us a thing. We just have to wait!" he insists into the receiver.

Then he sees me. He turns away to avoid meeting my gaze. After he hangs up he looks at me, despair written on his face.

"Did you hear what I said on the phone?"

"Yes."

He rubs his brow with the back of his hand. "How can you stay so calm at a time like this?"

"I'm not calm," I tell him. "But you can't lose sight of reason."

He looks at me bitterly. "Don't talk to me about reason."

Guilt

We meet at the same café in the rotunda in the park where we've been meeting for the past five months. We used to meet at this very same café fifteen years ago, when we were young. I had been incapable of expressing my feelings for her then, and she, though attracted to me, had misunderstood my silence. There's something both obvious and absurd about choosing to meet here now: a repetition that is both cyclical and maniacal, as unquestionably circular as the very roof over our heads.

"When do you think we can be together again?" she asks, adding quickly, "I'm sorry, but I have to ask. I think I have the right to know."

Tears come to her eyes; her expression is tormented yet determined. It is the most complicated of moments, the kind she feels offer her the chance to overcome both herself and her enemy.

"You mean *there*?" I ask, trying to gain time.

"Of course. What do you think?"

There is a studio apartment on the top floor of a nondescript building on Viale Campania with no doorman and no name on

the buzzer. It has low sloping ceilings and looks out on a landscape of rooftops. We started paying rent on it three months ago.
We'd meet there at the oddest hours, whenever we could, in the
morning when it was my free day at school and any time she
could get away from her family.

"I did what you said; I haven't gone there since last time,"
she says slowly. "Even though I honestly can't see any connection between what has happened and us."

It's a prepared speech. She's moving delicately through pre-
viously explored terrain.

"It's been almost a month now. You could have asked me
how I felt about it," she says.

"I thought I knew."

"You should have asked." The trepidation in her voice intro-
duces one of those discussions I so fear. "It's hard for me too, you
know. I have two children. My situation is very complicated."

"I know."

"I felt rejected by you. What did I do wrong?"

"You're not the guilty one," I say.

"Guilty?" She blanches with anger. "Go on, say it!"

"I just did."

"I'm warning you, don't talk to me like that!"

"Lower your voice! People will hear you," I whisper.

The woman at the next table who has been watching us
turns away.

"Why should I? I know exactly what's going to happen to us!
You, victim of your own guilt, and me, somehow part of it too!"

"I don't have the guilty conscience you think I do," I say to
her in a low voice. "Nor do I go to analysis to free myself of one.
It might work for you, but my story is different."

"How?" She looks at me, her eyes brimming with tears.

"My guilt is not imaginary, like yours. Mine doesn't stem

from childhood traumas, nor is it rooted in my unconscious. I'm guilty on several counts."

"Like what? The baby was born this way because of the doctors' mistakes, not yours!"

"I made mistakes too."

"When?"

"When she was pregnant and you reappeared in my life."

"I knew you'd say it was my fault! I could have bet on it," she says bitterly.

"I'm not talking about you. I'm talking about me." She waits for me to go on. "If I had been more present, maybe things would have been different."

She is startled. "Where, at the hospital? What could you have done? You couldn't have changed anything!"

"No, before. During the pregnancy. I'm referring to how upset she was about us."

She clutches the metal armrests of the chair.

"You told me she didn't know!"

"She guessed." I'm not sure if that's completely true; it just comes to me.

"All you do is lie—to her and to me!"

"The doctors asked her whether she suffered during the pregnancy."

"What did she say?"

"She said no, but I think she said it to protect me."

"I'm amazed by how much you've hidden from me!" she says angrily. "Why are you saying this now, to make yourself feel better?"

"No, because I need to know if it had any effect on the baby. The doctors don't rule it out."

"Did they say anything specifically?" she asks uneasily.

"No, just in general."

"They say all kinds of things! Don't torture yourself like this." Then, with the streak of brutality that has always surprised me, coming from that youthful face of hers, she adds, "Think about babies born in wartime."

I have no reply. Ours has been a kind of war: a war of suspicion and betrayal, with traps and defeats, located somewhere between tenderness, hate, and fear.

"You think that by confessing you'll be able to make amends," she says. "But you have to look at things differently. You're not as guilty as you would believe. You share the guilt."

"With whom—you?"

"No, her."

"Is that what your analyst would have you believe?"

Colleagues

A colleague of mine, a teacher of math and physics, recently had a growth removed from his armpit. The operation seems to have made him particularly forthcoming on medical matters. He asks me about Paolo. I tell him the baby's been discharged, the tremors have ceased, and though there is no local epileptic center—he devours my every word—the cortex has suffered some indirect damage. Still, according to the pediatrician who's been following his case, the symptoms may never come back. The case studies are reassuring, though there is a slight chance that the symptoms will return briefly during adolescence.

"Never again!" he exclaims, shaking his finger in a gesture that is both threatening and prophetic. "You'll never be able to rest easy again. There'll always be this sword of Damocles over your head!"

I look at him in bewilderment. I don't know how to react. I don't understand what he's trying to tell me. And yet it really is quite simple.

"Once there have been cerebral lesions, even indirectly,

there will always be"—and here he shakes his finger again—
"the risk of a seizure."

"Thank you for telling me," I say, in a voice not my own.

"Not at all, my friend," he says. "I know it seems harsh, but
it's always better to know things than to ignore them."

"Yes, of course," I reply.

My eyes glaze over. I head for the door. I'll never forget this,
I think to myself. And, in fact, I never have.

The Crystal Ball

It's an image favored by doctors who say they don't have one when they really don't want to comment on the future. "If only I had a crystal ball!" they say with a sigh, frowning in what they think of as wise perplexity. Or, rudely and authoritatively, they'll say, "We don't use crystal balls, you know!"

For years I hated them all. They hide behind a metaphor that's been worn thin through overuse, drained of all meaning, even with regard to the fantastic. It's as if they need to protect themselves from what they see as irrational demands, when actually they're calls for help from people who crave hope, people who'd like to escape into the future in order to liberate themselves from the torment of the present. Instead, these doctors choose to fall back on a phrase they probably first heard in medical school. (How they treasure the fatuities of the great!) Meanwhile, the alibi of professional ethics masks any eventual discontinuity in what they say. Not that the patients or their relatives actually believe in the crystal ball. They don't see it as the key to the future. For them it reflects their need to avoid painful self-analysis in order to be confronted with the details of the difficulties that lie ahead. Those doctors who are both competent and compassionate enough to address these issues have never regretted doing so.

I remember the doctor who, when Paolo was three months old, told us the truth: or what he really thought. He reflected at length before speaking. The room was fraught with tension. He didn't mention a crystal ball. A far greater expert in questions both of medicine and of humanity than so many of his colleagues, he looked at us and said gently, "I cannot tell you what your son will be like when he grows up. I can only make a few reasonable hypotheses.

"The most optimistic one: The cerebral damage caused by the forceps and a lack of oxygen at birth will be assimilated, leaving no subsequent trace. His condition could be marginal. This is not the most probable hypothesis.

"The median hypothesis: The cerebral lesions, though not deep, have damaged his language and motor skills. The child will begin speaking late; at age three he'll know a hundred words where another child might know a thousand. He won't be able to walk properly. His fine motor skills will be imperfect. His intelligence will be intact, yet he will seem immature because of his incomplete experience.

"The third and most negative hypothesis: The encephalogram doesn't reveal the degree of the lesions. It's still too early. The effects on his mobility and intelligence will be greater than suspected. In my opinion, this is the least probable hypothesis.

"However, I might be wrong. You will have to learn to live from day to day. Try not to think too much about the future. It will be a difficult experience, yet you will not regret it. You will be the better for it.

"These children are born twice. They have to learn to get by in a world that their first birth made difficult for them. Their second birth depends on you, on what you can give them. Because they are born twice, their journey through life is a far more agonizing one than most. Yet ultimately their rebirth will be yours too. This, at least, has been my experience. I have no more to tell you."

Thirty years later, I want to say thank you.

The First Appointment

The physiotherapist greets us in a dark, dismal, and uncomfortably small waiting room. Some houses, like some people, reveal the worst of themselves at the threshold and only later manage to correct that initial impression. As Oscar Wilde said, only the superficial don't trust their first impressions.

Taking turns holding the baby, we manage to remove our coats. Then, with our backs pressed against the wall, we open a dark closet and hang them up. We move into the rehabilitation room. It has hardwood floors, and its walls are lined with cushioned bumpers. There's a square gymnastics mat in the center. The gray foggy light of late afternoon filters through the window.

She motions for us to sit down on a wicker sofa, while she sinks down onto an oversized pillow on the floor. You can tell that's where she feels most comfortable.

She'd forgotten to tell us her fee over the telephone, so she promptly informs us. It's remarkably high. Slightly embarrassed, she observes our reactions, which we manage to hide with ease for once.

"Is that all right?" she asks.

"Yes," I reply.

There's something vaguely unpleasant about her manner. She seems nervous and awkward, almost foreign, simultaneously hesitant and aggressive. I realize this now, years later. But at the time, fearing the uncertainty of the results of the medical tests and overanxious to be reassured, I was primarily concerned with not upsetting the mood of the oracle, even if I did intuit some sense of her limitations. So much needs to be said—and in such a wide range of tenses! It takes years to answer things adequately, even ideally. And by then the interlocutor might have died or disappeared or simply have forgotten the question. Very few people actually have those lightning reactions that correspond with future memories. Nor can we who are disoriented with doubt or stupefied with surprise ever hope to imitate them.

The physiotherapist asks us to tell her clearly about Paolo's condition. I think she's afraid I'll give her too many details or be long-winded, because as soon as I start talking, she urges me on. "Yes, I see—yes," she says, negating all my efforts at dialogue. So instead I simplify and abbreviate and condense things. I conclude, in exasperation, by gesturing to Franca to pass her the baby.

The woman gathers him into her arms with maternal rapaciousness, as if it were a salvation. She lays him down on his back on the mat, extends his arms out to his sides, caresses his small hands, and tickles the soles of his feet. In time, I will come to see these actions repeated by many specialists, but now they seem knowing, graceful, expert. She asks us which doctor referred us to her. None of them, I tell her. What do you mean? she asks. A colleague of mine had heard of her, I say. What did the neurologist tell you? We don't have a neurologist; Paolo was discharged from the hospital a month after he was born. The doctors said his problems would eventually go away.

"Are they crazy?" she says, getting up onto her knees.

"No, not at all," Franca replies, turning pale. "We came to you for confirmation."

The physiotherapist looks at her in amazement.

"Just to be sure," Franca repeats, growing alarmed.

"But this child has brain damage!" she exclaims. "He has dystonic spastic quadriparesis! You didn't mention that!"

My legs go weak.

"This is not a passing phase," she continues. "We have to begin immediately!"

"Begin what?" I ask, wide-eyed.

"Physiotherapy! Several hours a day! You'll have to work with him constantly!" She turns to Franca, whose total silence betrays her panic. "We can't waste any more time!"

"What kind of problems will he have?" I ask apprehensively.

"Too many to list," she replies. "Besides, it depends on the evolution of his symptoms."

"For example?"

"The way he walks," she says, "might be irregular."

"How?"

"Like this," she replies, standing up. She's barefoot. She begins to walk slowly, like an overweight ballerina, swaying drunkenly from side to side until she loses her balance and falls to the floor.

"Understand?"

"Yes," I whisper.

It's a horrible image. I look at Franca. She has covered her mouth with her hand in shock.

"You're sure about that," I say in a monotone, uncertain if I'm questioning or confirming what she has just shown us.

"No, I'm not sure," she says, getting to her feet again and starting to walk with erratic movements, as if she were crossing a bed of white-hot coals. "His speech might be affected too, as well as his manual skills."

"What about his intelligence?" I ask, looking downward.

"No, I don't think so," she says. "There will be other, different problems."

I lean back. Franca dabs at her eyes with her handkerchief.

"Really? Nobody told you?" she asks.

"Someone in the clinic did, at the beginning," I say, "but they never mentioned it again."

"Amazing," she says, turning away, stunned.

I look over at Franca in silence.

On our way downstairs we carefully analyze the various aspects of the meeting, beginning with a list of her faults. The final result is both discomforting and reassuring.

"When did she say we should call her back?" I ask Franca.

"In two weeks."

"Will you?"

"No," she says, sure of our shared reaction. "She's far too catastrophic. No one ever mentioned these things to us. We can't trust her. We have to be able to trust the person who's treating our child."

"I agree. Besides, she doesn't have much experience. She's just starting out."

"Right."

. . .

Now, when I watch Paolo stagger off ahead of me, I recall seeing her stagger across the mat in that gray room at sunset, her shadow projected on the wall. She was the only person whose vision of the future resembled reality. Maybe that's why we chose to reject her.

What Is Normal?

What is normal? Nothing. Who is normal? No one.

When we're hurt by diversity, our first reaction is to deny its existence, not to accept it. We do so by denying normality. We say it doesn't exist. The spoken words suddenly seem distant, smug, sarcastic. When talking about normality, we resort to written language: "Normal people, quote unquote" or "so-called normal people."

Subjected to rigorous analysis no less frequently than diversity, normality reveals its inadequacies, fissures, deficiencies, lapses, shortcomings, and anomalies. Everything becomes an exception. Our need for the norm, if shooed away from the door, returns to menace us at the window. And it returns doubly dangerous, like a virus that has outstripped the medicines supposed to kill it. It's not by denying the existence of difference that we can fight it, but by modifying our image of the norm.

. . .

When Einstein was asked for passport information and chose to reply by saying "member of the human race," he wasn't ignoring our differences. He was dismissing them in a vaster manner, accepting and transcending them.

This is the landscape that needs to extend before us, both for those who make differentiation into discrimination and for those who try to avoid discrimination by entirely denying the existence of difference.

The Art Institute

For several years I taught at the Art Institute. I started working there when I was twenty-eight—it was my first position in a public high school—and I had never met a disabled person. Nowadays, you see a lot of them. I'm not sure if it's because I notice them more or because their number has increased. Probably a combination of both.

There was a girl in one of my classes who always sat in the front row. She had long blond hair, broad shoulders, and a round face; her body exuded strength and agility. She reminded me of an Australian swimmer who has just finished practice. She had bright eyes and a serene expression. She'd follow my lesson entranced, virtually hypnotized.

The first time I call her up to my desk to quiz her, she stands erect and composed, her hands behind her back. I can't hear what she's saying.

"Can you speak up, please?" I ask.

She bites her lip and shakes her head, as if I have asked her to do something impossible.

I look at her in amazement. She turns toward the class for help. Some of the students snicker. Then she turns back to me and starts to whisper. I beckon her closer, cupping my ear, making the sign that deaf people use. (I'll leave the more correct term of "hearing impaired" to those who are not familiar with the handicap.) She leans over in embarrassment and whispers, "I'm sorry. I can't speak any louder."

"Don't worry," I say boldly, "you're doing fine."

I'm not much older than she. I feel accessible, generous, liberal, correct. I'm a brilliant young teacher, living up to expectations. The students chuckle among themselves. Some of them even double over with laughter; others just sit there gaping and grinning.

I ask the girl questions that require short answers: names, dates, titles, places, basic notions (not an insignificant exam by any standard, as will become apparent when they're eventually abolished). For her part, she responds perfectly. And she's genuinely surprised by the transformation in my method.

I dismiss her with a smile. Beads of perspiration have gathered on my forehead. She was well prepared and deserves a high grade, which I proceed to write down in the register with a flourish so it is evident to her. I have become a minor hero of modern didactic methods; I am both helpful and detached. Even the rest of the class seems to think so, having passed from laughter to smiles of appreciation, no small feat indeed.

As she is sitting down again, tired and happy, the student next to her tells me she has an easier time with the more technical subjects, where she has to speak less. It's harder with Professor Cornali, apparently, who teaches Art History. This girl speaks freely and candidly, while the blond girl and the rest of the class nod in agreement; she has become my informant, a kind of representative or envoy.

"Why is it harder with Professor Cornali?" I ask.

"He says he's deaf," she replies, smiling bitterly.

Her classmates mumble their skepticism.

"His hearing is fine," she adds. "He does it to be hard on her."

The truth probably lies somewhere in the middle, I think. Professor Cornali may be a little deaf and the girl might make things hard for him, which he counteracts by being hard on her.

"I'll look into it," I say.

I did. As Horace says, in the middle lies virtue, not truth. Had it been otherwise, the problem would have been solved long ago. But the truth, whatever it may be, is always something else.

Cornali doesn't have hearing problems. He has problems with his students. In this regard he's no different from the rest of us. Who would ever deny it? No, it's true, some people would, but they belong to a class of blissful idiots who go on TV proclaiming things like "Life has given me everything I could possibly hope for"—fine people, if only they weren't so arrogant, always hoping to arouse envy in others for their imagined lives.

In particular, Cornali has problems with people with problems. Disabled people can arouse all sorts of reactions among normal people. Just think of Hahnemann's nineteenth-century principle of "like cures like," the basis for homeopathic medicine. Cure the weak with the weak. I've seen it applied to human relations again and again; it can be both frightening and illuminating. For example, if a disabled child inadvertently gets mixed in with a group of normal children, people will respond with curiosity, amazement, or dismay, depending on the degree of cruelty in their point of view. The only people capable of withholding judgment and retaining a more ambiguous view are those willing to see in the child a reflection of themselves. Others, overwhelmed with fear at the mere suggestion of such a notion, take refuge in escapism; still others, in aggression. And yet they will have to return to it, their dark destiny, their downfall. That one neurosis attracts, intensifies, and appeases another is a fact that is easily proved in the endurance of many marriages.

Cornali took immediate aim at the girl. He faked his every effort to hear her—or so my informant told me during our hallway conversations, amid passing glances and knowing nods from her fellow students—and instead asked her at length about the cause and details of her disorder, thereby managing to aggravate it. When pretending not to hear her he'd lean forward over the lectern, but always at a distance. He never let her speak into his ear. The one time she moved toward him, he pushed her violently away and she burst into tears.

I discover what I should have known all along: All the teachers, depending on their subjects, have a problem with the girl, but everyone has found a way around it. This attenuates the pride I took in my own versatility. To be *primus inter pares* never satisfied an ambition, especially when "equals" includes everyone else. The only exception is Cornali.

Once he sat next to me during a midyear faculty meeting in which we were discussing the students' grades. "Can you hear anything she says?" he whispers to me, when her name is called out.

"Yes, everything," I reply.

"What do you mean, everything?" he says. "Then I must be deaf!"

"Maybe you are," I say, glancing quickly at him.

"No, really! I'm serious. Tell me the truth. You only hear a part of what she says."

"I hear almost everything."

I cover myself by saying *almost*, thereby conserving the credibility of *everything*.

He shakes his head. "I'm not going to pass her."

"Why not?"

"Because I can't hear a word she says," he replies flatly. "I suppose I'm limited."

"That's for sure."

"We all have our limits. You have yours and I have mine."

"Can't you try and overcome them?"

"I've tried, believe me," he says, with some regret. "But I just can't." After a pause, he adds, "It's a real shame."

"What is?"

"To have that defect. I don't know what to call it—whether it's cerebral palsy, asphyxia, extreme shyness, or some other kind of emotional block."

"You know what the real shame is?" I say, staring straight ahead of me at the iron fixtures on the window. "To have a brain like yours."

I hear him breathe in sharply but he doesn't reply. Then he says—and I'm not sure if it's a question or a threat—"You're joking, aren't you?"

"No. I'm not joking," I reply. "I might be exaggerating, though."

To discourage anger in others they say you should stay calm.

"The real tragedy," I go on to say, "is the brain itself. Even

Christ said it: Evil is what comes out of the mouth, not what goes into it."

"Could you please leave Christ out of this?" he hisses. "I can't stand your talking to me like that."

Actually, people can stand an infinite number of things, even when they deny it. He doesn't scare me; I'm twice as big as he is. I hear my pulse hammering in my brain. My mouth is dry. I retreat a little bit.

"I didn't mean to offend you," I say quietly, as if confiding in him. "I just don't like being thought of as old-fashioned. You accuse me of it continuously. If I'm old-fashioned, what are you?"

It's always a good idea to pretend you're being attacked when you're really the one doing the attacking. He takes advantage of the alibi I've offered him and moderates his tone.

"I think you're too demanding."

"What about you? What do you expect from a handicapped student?"

That was probably the first time I ever used the adjective that was destined to condition my life. I fear I've spoken it with a flourish, the way people do who are not directly affected by it (politicians and intellectuals make a grand show of this). He reacts with brutal nonchalance.

"What do you mean, handicapped? She's just immature! You can tell by her behavior. We mustn't coddle students who have weaknesses; we must encourage them to overcome them!"

The principal peers over his glasses at us from the head of the table. He's a quiet and patient person, an expert on Zanella, six months away from retirement. Forty-three years of experience have taught him that, in the dictum "respect for discipline," one word is superfluous: discipline. Respect would be enough.

"Excuse us," I say.

He nods, adjusting his glasses on the bridge of his nose.

I notice that my use of the indirect object "us" has had a mitigating effect on Cornali, if only grammatically. Actually, grammar has a far greater effect on that which remains obscure in our unconscious than is generally assumed.

"I'm sorry I spoke like that," I whisper almost imperceptibly, in a voice not unlike the girl's.

He nods. Maybe he doesn't want to reply. Maybe he just doesn't want to disturb the principal.

"Forgive me," I add.

He bites his lip, pensive. I assume he feels compensated, spared a future exchange of hostilities. Then I make a mistake.

"What grade are you going to give her?" I ask.

"An F."

The struggle to save the girl from Cornali's sentence went on for several more months. (I will now shift into the past tense, which in my own personal grammar I usually reserve for historic events.) It was inserted into a broader context—a slanderous campaign by Cornali against my teaching methods.

More than anything else, Cornali considered himself a harbinger of the new pedagogy. The very same man who could humiliate a person, already humiliated by fate, by pretending he was deaf committed himself to the fight for students' rights. He proposed and achieved—though not without the tacit opposition of those of us who were more sensitive to the issue— the abolition of the formal manner of address. A lot of people believe that equality should be reflected in pronoun usage, and they're not entirely wrong. It's just that the same people who fight for it are often the same people who'd like to see grammar done away with altogether.

By asking his students to consider him their contemporary, Cornali, given the thirty-year age difference, made them feel uncomfortable. He was like one of those parents who profess to be their children's best friend and deceive themselves into believing that they can share in both their games and their age.

Cornali's next step was to let the students decide their own grades. I had abandoned a similar experiment during my second year of teaching as soon as I realized how dangerous it could be. The humbler students, leaning toward self-effacement, gave themselves lower grades than they deserved while the shrewder ones gave themselves stellar ones. In the end, we were all dissatisfied, both the students and I. Cornali, meanwhile, ideologue that he was, dispensed altogether with the experimental phase and passed on to the corrected version. He raised all their grades—both the chaste Lenten grades of the serious students and the overgenerous grades of the less deserving ones. His students, geniuses and hidden talents each and every one of them, were practically euphoric. He told me about it one day, while comparing our classes.

"You see," he began, in that composed and meditative way that is so typical of the passive-aggressive, "you address your students formally and I can understand that. You're much younger than I am. You need to put distance between yourself and them. But then you make the mistake of interpreting that as a sign of authority. I, on the other hand, at my age, can address them informally. I don't have to simulate authority. I have it, and I choose to relinquish it."

He had one of those minds that was constantly in flux. Ideas would simmer together, come to a boil, and then flow uncontrollably over the edge while he, their chef, would look on carelessly. Taken one at a time, the ingredients might have been savory, but together the mixture was unpalatable.

"I can tell that discipline is important to you," he added. "You're so uptight! Discipline is nothing but the last vestige of an authoritarian system."

"No," I insisted, "it's the other way around. The chaos in your classroom is a sign of authoritarianism: Whoever has the loudest voice dominates. I expect silence so that when I explain something or when someone has a question, the others can hear. If not, they can go elsewhere."

"Don't you see how old-fashioned you are?" he asked in amazement, as if he had discovered a criminal. "You expect total silence."

"Of course I do," I said. "Like a pianist, I need silence to play so others can hear."

"What surprises me most," he concluded soberly, "is that the students actually respect you despite the fact that you are so demanding."

He looked up at me, stupefied, radiantly confused. He couldn't begin to conceive that this was precisely why my students listened to me.

"Why, of course!" he exclaimed. "It makes perfect sense! Authority—the recognized state of superiority that Horkheimer talks about—doesn't need a pretext!"

What about those who don't have authority? I thought to myself. What do they do?

Both his twisted sense of logic and his partial reasoning, which he considered complete, generated new misunderstandings between us. He enjoyed discrediting me in front of other teachers by saying I had made listeners out of the students by relying on a false sense of egalitarianism, not by threats or punitive measures. Essentially, he encouraged undiscipline, and he'd rage against those teachers who didn't know how to deal with it.

"One more reason to guarantee it to them," I'd object. "If teachers don't know how to take charge of their students, do you really think they should be left at their mercy?"

"That's their problem," he'd say, with a glint in his eye.

"What about their subjects? Who will learn them?"

"No one," he'd reply boldly.

And that's precisely what happened. It wasn't his future, so he didn't worry about it. (That's the cynical truth about him that I have come to accept over the years, even if *cynical* isn't generally used to describe someone who embodies a behavior but rather a person who repudiates one.)

Hordes of students abandoned their classes, both materially and figuratively. Walking down the hall, you could hear the teachers shouting, either for silence or simply to make themselves heard above the din. And it was only when the students were ready to let these exasperated and shrill commands have an effect on them that the teachers would gain an audience.

Rather than being on the students' side, Cornali was primarily against his fellow teachers. His divining rod for wrong causes led him to ignore the more important reasons for siding with a generation in revolt, even if we only felt its muffled, distant rumblings at our school. My own position on things—at some times of alliance, at other times of dissent—seemed more like a question of prudent strategy to him than the issue of choice that it actually was. Once he even accused me of being intelligent. Another time he scolded me for my analytic capacity, a typical retort for someone who doesn't have the most basic grasp of things. His greatest contribution to the reformation of the education system at our school was to assist in the dissolution of order. I don't know what the situation is like now, because I stopped teaching long ago, but I'm tempted to believe that, in this light, things are actually worse than they were. While lack of discipline might have been seen as revolutionary then, today it is part of the institution. Nowadays the best teachers manage to neutralize the situation by dedicating themselves to the task at hand, but they constitute the minority. The other teachers, abandoned in high seas, act as one would imagine — they try to lighten their load. They expect less of their students and yet, judging from the amount of bureaucratic paperwork, the sancta sanctorum of the new system, they manage to obtain more. There's no better way to raise the profit level of a class than by lowering the yardstick of success, a compromise that the mortified teachers keep to themselves and the inexperienced students do not notice. This is what I've gathered from the more forthcoming teachers, unless I make the wrong kind of friends.

Cornali, who fought for the abolition of a grade for conduct (a notion that the future itself would make superfluous), decided to implement a change in the structuring of his course. He decided to study the retrogressive history of art, from the twentieth century back to the Stone Age. It was like telling someone that they'd get somewhere faster if they walked backward. At first the students were attracted by the novelty. Then they realized it would actually take them longer to study in this way, as they frequently had to stop and examine things in both directions. But by then it was too late to go back to the old system.

"I don't like making comparisons," he'd say, in the manner of someone who's about to do just that, "but your class obeys you; mine follows me. You invoke fear in your students; I arouse sympathy. I make them feel like geniuses; you make them feel like laborers."

I'd listen to him in amusement. There was a genuine warmth in the geyser of his ideas; it was his most sympathetic trait. He considered himself "a creative type" and loved to remind you of it. He'd propose the most improbable hypotheses and then erase them with a wave of his hand, as if they were the pure follies of genius. A passage from the Veda, a phrase by Lao Tzu, a saying by Confucius: all added a hint of orientalism to his words—at least that was the intent. Indeed, as long as you didn't dwell on what he was saying, the effect was of lightness. As with many so-called "creative types," he was far more interested in the creative act than in the creation itself, although he did expect applause for the latter (and it was never lacking). In his uniqueness he was a product in a series. He was typical of our society but didn't know it. He probably would have been horrified to see his image reflected in someone else, an experience that life had spared him.

"It takes nine months for a baby to grow," I'd remind him bleakly. "School lasts nine months. At the end of the year we'll see who's right."

"How will you know?"

"The students: They'll let us know."

Toward the end of the year, just before the final faculty meeting in which we were to announce our grades, the maestro had his coup de théâtre. He told every student what grade they'd be receiving and explained the curve on which it was based. He gave the lowest grades to the best students (for not making full use of their talents) and the highest grades to the weakest students (as a reward for their efforts).

The students reacted as anyone, except the prophet himself, could have guessed: with complete silence. It was an emotional catastrophe. Aware of my issues with Cornali, the students came to me for comfort. They came in dismay and despair and with lowered heads. The best students in the group didn't know how to react to the injustice of being ranked below the average ones. Cornali had figured—with the blinkered imagination of all ideologues—that they would be insensitive to grades. But to find a young person insensitive to grades is about as hard as finding one who's insensitive to money. As for the weaker students, Cornali had thought they would have been ecstatic to receive the coveted grades. While good grades would certainly have pleased them, marks of excellence made them feel ashamed, as though they had been acknowledged as complete failures, beyond hope or measure. The most deluded of them all was Cornali himself, who was amazed that the younger generation hadn't generated a man genetically different from his own.

Cornali's vision of history had led him to imagine modern man like one of those extraterrestrial monsters with an enormous cranium and spindly legs. The head needed to be large so it could accumulate the experience of millennia, while the body replicated the fragility of a child. To discover, instead, that they had to begin all over again each time made him see in the twilight the world that others see in the dawn.

The most disconcerting thing about Cornali's behavior at the close of that turbulent year was his visible anger toward the girl. The energy with which he fought for the rights of the disabled was matched only by the hostility with which he persecuted her. And yet he saw no contradiction in this. He was convinced that the girl wasn't disabled. He was reluctant to believe in mental illness altogether, perhaps because he felt threatened by it. Instead, he insisted she couldn't overcome her problems by reason alone because she was inherently weak, lazy, or indecisive. Cornali suffered from seeing things in a doubly distorted manner: he thought her symptoms were voluntary choices and he believed that punitive measures could rid her of her troubles forever.

Getting to know Cornali through school motivated me to reflect at length on the theme of contradiction. I came to the conclusion that, despite everything, contradictions don't really exist. That is, they exist only on a mathematical-logical plane. It's undeniably true that people say one thing and do another, yet they never see that as contradictory. Both good people and criminals alike resort to the principle of contradictions to justify their mistakes, but ultimately their behavior can be completely understood only if one casts aside that very principle. One must look at the agency that compels things to happen, at the ungraspable coherence behind things, at the unknowable totality. Then those actions no longer seem contradictory but necessary, and the whole principle of contradictions is absurd.

I'm not talking about a Cartesian form of reasoning here. Nor am I referring to the world of dreams, where travelers lose and find themselves again. Rather, what I'm alluding to is that mysterious and obscure nucleus known as the individual and what rouses him or her to speed.

The girl understood that Cornali, by defending the disabled in general and yet simultaneously attacking her, was not a victim of contradictions, but that he was bending them to his will. In order to obtain his desired result he used the basest and most efficient weapon: reason. Ultimately, he got what he wanted.

She refused to answer him; she shut herself into a guilty, impenetrable state of mutism. He told me about it triumphantly. He saw it as the definitive confirmation of her immaturity. It's odd that the concept of maturity is most frequently invoked by the immature. Here too, things only seem contradictory. In reality, by accusing others of being immature, such people actually defend themselves.

The girl gave up studying for Cornali's class during the last month of school. She continued to attend his lectures, though, perhaps because he was one of the few teachers who could still manage to hold them. I don't want to contradict myself—fatal verb—but Cornali did have a fine mind, blinded as much by intelligence as by idiocy. He fought hard so that disabled people could come to school at a time when they were simply being turned away. It was the first time, albeit surrounded by oppression and violence, that we radically faced the problem of integration. This fact should not be ignored or forgotten, especially now, when each occasion for passing judgment spurs new inequalities and discriminations.

When the girl's name was called at the final faculty meeting of the year, Cornali didn't say a word. The rest of us spoke up on her behalf, but he remained silent. The principal, who in his formal manner sought to conserve the final vestiges of authority, turned patiently toward him.

"Please be so kind as to give us your assessment," he said.

"D," Cornali replied.

The Photograph

"Don't move!" I say.

He's holding on to the pole of the beach umbrella, his arms are stiff, his feet are planted deep in the sand, his body bends at a hypotenuse angle. He's starting to slip; his mouth contorts in pain. He falls backward onto the sand, the palms of his hands spread wide open.

"Let's try it a different way."

I turn him over onto his stomach so he's lying in the same position as the eighty-year-old woman on the lounge chair next to us and proceed to cover his back with sand. Her skin is covered with wrinkles, partly from old age, partly because of the sun. She's sure that the sun is the source of good health; she thinks the more it seeps into her thick hide, the closer she will be to immortality. She dies a year later, looking as shriveled as a furnace-dried centipede.

"Rest your chin in your hands," I suggest.

He tries, but his elbows slip out sideways and his head droops down onto the sand.

I help him back into the pose but by the time I bring the camera up to my eye his head has already fallen forward again.

"You'll never get him to stay like that," Franca says, picking him up and wiping off the sand. "It would be hard for us too."

Now there's a phrase that comes up repeatedly among those who assist the handicapped: *us* used as a term of comparison, a symbol of a supreme normality, an unreachable—and all too common—finishing line.

"Why do you insist on photographing him like that?" she asks.

I'm not really sure. I was thinking about cherubs, the way they lean on their elbows at the corners of Renaissance paintings. Why do I have to search for such absurd and remote models?

I sit him down in the sand and dig a hole around him. He falls forward. His face gets dirty. He doesn't cry because he knows I'm responsible for his troubles. Instead, he looks at me with a mixture of disapproval and benevolence. Sometimes he's almost fatherly with me; it's one of his qualities that touches me deeply.

I brush him off and sit him down with his legs crossed like a little Buddha.

"There—stay like that—don't move!"

I sound just like my father, one of the few vacationers before the war to own a legendary Zeiss, when he used to take pictures of me on the hills above Lake Como.

The little Buddha wavers unsteadily for a moment before losing his balance and falling forward. I snap the picture just as he turns his frightened face toward mine. In the photograph he comes out looking serious and worried. Normal.

"That one!" Franca says, picking it out from the rest and slipping it under the glass frame that now hangs in the hallway.

The Brother

Families know how to defend themselves against their enemies. They foster a sense of danger in much the same way the city of ancient Rome, according to Sallust, fostered fear among its citizens in order to bolster internal strength. But then they discover the enemy at home. Paolo has an enemy. It's his brother.

Alfredo is three years older than Paolo. He has an enemy too. Before Paolo's birth he was the only child. He didn't have to share his parents with a rival. He was king.

What gives him away? His laughter. Laughter reveals so much about us, so much more than tears. Many animals cry, but besides anthropoid apes, as far as I know, very few laugh. Then there are humans.

Alfredo laughs for reasons that are often unclear. If his brother tries to walk from one side of the hallway to the other, he'll laugh from the doorway of his bedroom. When Paolo couldn't cry, when he could only sob, making him gasp for air (it's horrible when a person can't cry), Alfredo would explode into convulsive laughter.

"Nervous laughter," Franca would say, updating an expression that she probably learned in her youth. Once, nerves were the unconscious. "It's his nerves," they'd say about someone afflicted with neuroses. "A nervous breakdown," they'd say when he fell prey to the inner enemy. And, "crazy," they'd say when he lost it completely.

I began to be suspicious of Alfredo's laughter.

He'd laugh when his brother would trip. "Idiotic laughter," Franca would say, in a variation on the theme. But when I told her what I thought, she said that everyone laughs when a person trips.

"At the movies, maybe," I replied.

"No, in real life. We're all sadists."

This conclusion, presented so compellingly and universally, managed to confuse me. But on another occasion, when Paolo tripped on the stairs and Alfredo laughed, I turned to her and asked, "Why aren't *you* laughing?" She was disconcerted by my question but she replied by hiding behind the alibi that we usually reserve for children when they wound us—that they're young.

I couldn't stop thinking about it. I can understand not worrying about a minor incident: it's all right to be indifferent. But why laugh? Is it nervous laughter? Is it idiotic laughter? No, it's gleeful laughter. We laugh at the movies when the pompous fellow slips or when the tyrant is deposed or when the archenemy surrenders. The key is that the enemy has to fall.

Whenever Alfredo saw his brother the enemy in trouble, a fleeting, soulless smile would cross his face. Soon he was laughing more frequently. A sinister euphoria, a bitter *allegria*, gave him away. It happened with particular frequency when Paolo was learning how to tie his shoes. According to a book we

have on physical rehabilitation, learning to tie your shoes is
one of the most important conquests on the road to indepen-
dence. (I'm not sure if that's reassuring or disturbing to know,
but in any case it's precious for our pride.) It wasn't just his
heavy-handedness that made it difficult; his body weight made
him lose his balance and fall forward. Alfredo would watch him
struggle, spellbound. Once Franca walked into the room and
saw Alfredo laughing. "Why don't you help him? He's your
brother," she said. "Why should I? He has to learn on his
own," he had replied. People have infinite reasons for refusing
to help, but the cleverest one is precisely because they want to
help. "Help him!" Franca yelled, giving him a push and making
him fall down next to his brother.

What amazed me most was not that this form of hate had
been born but that it persisted. When I spoke to a psychiatrist
friend about it, she smiled gently and knowingly, as if she had
run into an old friend.

"It's really quite common," she said with a sigh. (It's always
reassuring to discover that our absurdities are normal. That's
how we cope with them.) "It's pure jealousy of the younger sib-
ling, who gets pampered by the parents and is always the center
of attention."

"Yes, but because of his problems."

"That makes no difference," she had replied. "Alfredo stopped
being the sun and became a satellite. He'll never be able to forgive his brother for that. That kind of wound never heals."

I've never been able to understand why the wounds of the
unconscious refuse to heal. All other wounds heal, but unconscious ones continue to bleed for as long as we live. Perhaps
because they're unconscious, because everybody knows about

them except us. Alfredo wasn't aware that he hated Paolo, at least on the surface. Once I described his brother's condition to him in great detail, comparing it with his.

"So?" he asked.

"So you have to help him," I said.

"Why? Don't I already?"

"No," I replied, "you do the exact opposite." I'll never forget how he cried, at first in a whimper and then with growing distress. The only way I could calm him down was by shaking him. "Think about it!" I had shouted in his face.

"That was the last thing you should have said," my psychiatrist friend comforted me by saying. "Only love can attenuate the wounds. Now you have to love him even more than before."

But I loved him less. That's what worried me. You can make practically anything happen except feelings. And still, those who are closest to you will continue to tell you what you should do and how you should behave. They construct logical systems and create mathematical proofs and come up with undeniable conclusions: If you love then you should react in such and such a way. But I feel differently. Franca is barely surprised by me anymore, while the other one can only accuse me. How many times did I pretend to react the way they expected me to? And while I know that mine was a fiction, can we be sure their proofs were flawless? That the reactions I simulated were the only "right" ones? Life is so much more than a proof. Anyway, they were the wrong reactions for me. Perhaps maturity means respecting the injustice of one's own reactions. Perhaps maturity means substituting the injustice of conventional thinking with unjust freedom. Even if this—I am beginning to realize—sounds like the introduction to a manual on criminal behavior.

. . .

Alfredo, who was not living up to my expectations, could have relied on the very same alibi. If he felt aversion toward his brother, was it really his fault? And wasn't I also not living up to his expectations of understanding and solidarity? The rationales of the weak make sense to us only when they become our own.

Alfredo had been dethroned and could not be resigned to that. To top it off, he didn't even like his brother. The frailty that should have made him feel more tenderly toward him—there's that *should* again—actually drove a stake between them. The pathology distanced him. His discomfort changed to repulsion. I knew what he was going through because sometimes I felt the same way.

This made it feel foreign to me. We're reluctant to accept those flaws that, magnified in others, we fear in ourselves. Because of the difference in scale and the accompanying sense of remorse, they become unacceptable. Alfredo would smirk when Paolo would try, and fail, to catch a ball. Then, when it happened a second time, he'd laugh. That's the difference between us: I'd get exasperated while he'd be amused. (There's never a lack of comparisons that favor us.) But Paolo, on the other hand, who stood between us, sometimes just couldn't take it anymore and would start to cry; his hands would grip at the smooth floor as if it too might slip away from him.

One on One

The principal of the elementary school is disabled. He limps
when he walks, dipping slightly with each step, his left leg
extending out to the side. When he sits down, he plants his cane
in front of him like a baseball bat and rests his chin on top of his
hands.

Writing about him now, after so many years, I realize that I
never knew—nor was I ever curious to know—the cause of his
impediment. It could have been the war. Maybe he had polio.
My general indifference, which is even more telling because of
my personal case, teaches me something about the distance that
exists between the disabled and us.

In any event, his impediment was eclipsed by his enormous
vitality. He'd get up from his desk suddenly, violently, rotating
his stiff leg outward. And when he came down the hall—tall,
bearded, and gaunt, hunched over his cane with that lopsided
gait of his—teachers and children alike would move aside to
let him by. And if someone didn't notice in time that he was
advancing toward them, they'd leap out of the way to avoid an

encounter. He was fully aware of the uneasy feelings he pro-
voked in others. Indeed, he often chose to intensify them by
waving his cane in the air to emphasize his words or to point
someone out, in both cases managing to transform a simple gesture into a threat.

I knew he was feared within the school as a serious womanizer.
All the female teachers had to defend themselves from his gruff
rapacity. From the older women he expected the smallest dis-
play of sexual loyalty, a kind of temporary and immediate relief.
Though somewhat more careful with the younger ones, he was
no less insistent. Once, called before the Superintendent after
being accused by one of his victims, he shamelessly managed to
have the charges reversed in the name of corruption. I'd like to
hope that today such a reversal wouldn't be possible and he
wouldn't be able to get away with it. But back then the victim
gave up trying, as she said, to nail him to his responsibilities. Nor
was there any lack of women either, among the so-called "non-
faculty staff" who had had some kind of intimate relationship
with him, an expression that in his case suggested something
sordid and lecherous.

This bristly-faced, smooth-talking city satyr was constantly
on the prowl for sexual favors, for pleasures stolen through
intimidation and surprise, for brief liaisons with women who
were at their wits' end in silent despair. He reminded me of
the pillager of a ruined city or a jackal after an earthquake. Or
of one of those men who'd be shot on the spot—now there's
an unparalleled expression (we find a variation of it in "sum-
mary execution"). It's a terminology that, under the guise of
"equality," always managed to satisfy my homicidal instincts.

It's a shame we can punish only those who commit physical crimes and not those who are guilty of psychological ones. I detest men who "collect" sexual adventures; they use trickery and deception to obtain that which rapists obtain with force. Moreover, these psychological rapists are considered great seducers. What distinguishes the two, besides the apparent identity of their object (never a better word) of desire, is that they are never won over by their prey, they're never taken with their victims' loss of power. These men court women with the same dark determination with which misogynists avoid them. Essentially, both groups hate women, only in different ways and with different consequences. That the scorn they have for their victims is matched by their victims' image of them validates them, provides them with the final stamp of approval. As such, the man finds the alibi to begin his hunt all over again.

The principal of the Martin Luther King Scuola Elementare might not have needed an alibi. He was only concerned about the penal repercussions. While psychological thieves are unquestionably of lower principles than apple thieves (the biblical fruit being the preferred one for such metaphors), no laws exist to stop them. Indeed, if their intentions are never transformed into action, a crime is never actually committed. This is the minuscule abyss that separates the penal from the moral code.

These prejudices were well established within me when I met with the principal in his office on the second floor of the recently completed school. Its structure—cube-shaped buildings connected by staircases, bridges, and open, airy corridors—and the outlying constellation of lawns and shrubs gave it a modern feeling of spaciousness and light, entirely different from the Lombrosian isolation of my own school.

His manner is both gruff and courteous. He wants to make me feel like a colleague. Given his seniority in age, he has the sad privilege of inviting me to address him with the informal *tu*. He observes me carefully. He has sunken cheeks and his eyes are bright with excitement. Pointing to his bad leg, which juts out from behind the desk, he refers to the unfair circumstances that unite us. There is a kind of caustic glee in this casual show of solidarity; it's the bitterly private sense of humor of someone who enjoys imposing his handicap on others.

"Now let's be clear," he says promptly.

I've always disliked that phrase. It's never the invitation to transparency that it seems to be. On the contrary, it always inaugurates an exchange of hostilities.

"You're lucky to have found a principal like me."

He looks up to see how I react to what he's saying.

"If there's anyone who knows what it means to be handicapped, it's me."

I nod, glancing discreetly at his leg.

"Your son will have everything he needs here: the right teacher, the right classroom on the ground floor. . . ."

I ought to be happy, and in fact I am. But something about this man reminds me of a tour guide or a real estate agent, extolling a product in order to justify its price. What price will I have to pay?

"You won't have to worry about a thing. Just transportation, that's all."

"That's not a problem; we'll bring him by car or he'll come in his go-cart," I assure him. "My wife will take care of that."

"Fine, but—" He stops himself, as if interrupted by a thought, as if he were considering me in light of an idea that flashed through his mind. But he held off. "You won't have to worry about a thing: lunch breaks, recesses, absences. I imagine your son requires special attention."

I hesitate for a moment.

"Yes," I say. "Better add it to the list."

"I'm giving you the best teacher I've got. A blond girl from Bolzano, Signorina Bauer. A very understanding person, though not with men."

He peers at me intensely.

"Do you like women? There's a pretty good choice here. Ah, if it weren't for this damn leg."

He extends it out farther, an expression of pain suddenly crossing his face.

"Still, I manage," he continues. "You know, I just can't do without it. Who was it that said it was as necessary to him as food itself? Well, the same goes for me." After a brief pause he adds, "My wife died ten years ago. It's better that way, poor thing. I really wasn't cut out for marriage."

Just then, the secretary must have looked in and signaled to him because he nods and she enters the room with a file and some papers for him to sign.

I look at him carefully. As he sits there against the light, a large plate-glass window behind him, his silhouette reminds me of the devil, come down from some craggy peak to reign over this glass palace.

"What are you thinking about?" he asks.

"Nothing," I lie (as one always does when answering like that). "No, actually"—I correct myself—"I was thinking about the impression I get of your school."

"Really? And what would that be?"

"That it's efficient, things get done. But people had already told me about it."

"Oh, really?" he asks, apprehensively curious.

"Yes," I say. "The only negative things I heard have to do with your adventures."

"Which ones?"

"Those with the opposite sex."

I don't think I've ever used that term before, suggestive of both evolutionism and isolationism. It's probably because of him. He looks at me in utter dejection.

"And you believe all that nonsense?"

"No. I'm just referring it to you."

He shrugs. "Water under the bridge. I never forced anyone to do anything. It's a free country, don't you think?"

"Of course."

"A few years ago I had some problems with a teacher, but she packed up and moved back to the country." His eyes flash with anger. "Poor thing."

He used the same words to describe his wife. (Where there's contempt for people, there's contempt for language.)

"What do you expect!" he says, gesturing toward the sky. "I'm just a little ship! I navigate by sight." Then, after a pause, he adds, "We have to distract ourselves somehow, don't you think? Life has been rough enough on us already. I know a thing or two about it." He scrutinizes me. "But you have your own troubles. There has to be some kind of compensation, don't you think?"

"Of course," I reply.

More than an associate, he's looking for an accomplice. And he finds one. We give up so easily in dialogue! And we're equally as inflexible in our monologues.

"You're not some kind of moralist, are you?" he suddenly asks suspiciously.

"No," I say with a smile. I could practically be his surrogate. "There's nothing worse than that."

"I agree."

When you have to find something to agree on, pretend to find it in words.

He observes me with curiosity. "I only ask because I have the impression that you and I will get along."

"Yes, I'm sure we will."

"You're at least twenty years younger than I, but intelligence has no age, right?"

"Absolutely," I say.

I'm using words that are not my own. It happens when people get the worst of you. It's usually a bad sign, for all parties involved.

"You'll see—your son will have everything he needs. He'll be surrounded by friends. I guarantee it."

"I'm very grateful to you."

"Oh, please." He sighs. "We've got to help each other out. I do something for you, you do something for me. Isn't that the way it works?"

"Absolutely," I say again.

Here it comes. I knew it had to come to this, I just didn't know when or how. The whole conversation has been gravitating toward this point.

"Come to think of it . . . there *is* something I wanted to ask you," he says quickly. "May I?" He looks up at me with some reservation, as if he too were surprised.

"Of course."

"You might know that I'm something of a dilettante poet. I say 'dilettante' and you know exactly what I mean: no grand ambitions, especially at my age. It might have been different when I was younger, but now . . ."

It occurs to me that dilettantes are the only ones to use that word. And perhaps it's only right to call them that since that's how they consider themselves.

"I've never had any high literary ambitions; I'll leave that to the professional intelligentsia."

I detect in his tone something aggressive and condescending, masked with indifference, typical among dilettantes toward those who are not.

"I've had my fair share of prizes: Il Gabbiano D'Oro, Il Premio Radici, all small-town things but then again I'm small-town too. Still, it's a pleasure to receive them."

"I know what you mean," I say animatedly. "They're the fairest prizes around these days."

"You're right about that!" he exclaims, eyes bright with fury. "Outside of all those literary games!"

I nod soberly. There are certain things you have to say about literary prizes, just as there are for weddings and funerals.

"That's where the real experts are—the real readers!" he adds. "Not the publishing elite!"

I can well imagine his tirade against editors. And theirs against him.

"In any case, I've accumulated quite a small capital of poems. Nothing remunerative, though." He smiles. "Still, I can't complain. Poetry is like women: all time gained, not lost. Don't you agree?"

I nod vaguely. It doesn't really matter if I agree or disagree. It matters that I communicate.

"That's right," he continues. "I can tell you agree with me." He sighs. "I'd like to publish a book of my poems, a collection, as they say. To give to my friends. They're the ones who keep insisting that I do it."

A common theme among dilettantes: the circle of friends who insist on publication. It may even be true. Nondilettantes (I'll refrain from using the high-risk term "professionals") usually have friends who prudently advise them *not* to publish.

"Then I'd send the book on to a more important prize. But I don't want to self-publish it. I want a good editor and a good publishing company. What do you think?"

"It sounds fair," I reply calmly, yet worried.

"Look! Here it is!" he says, with some degree of surprise, opening the top drawer of his desk. "I brought the manuscript with me to the office so I could have a look at it now and then during the day. You wouldn't know it, but I'm my very worst critic."

"I'm sure you are."

"I make corrections constantly. I'm never satisfied. I'm never sure if le mot juste, as the French used to say, is the right one. But I try!" He pulls a thick sheaf of papers held together with an elastic cord and protected by two sheets of red plastic out of the drawer. "Aren't you curious to see it?" he asks, placing it on the desk.

He passes it to me with the same rapid gesture with which a merchant passes goods across the counter to a client.

I pick it up with fake delicacy. It's called *One on One*.

"I'm not sure I'm the right person to judge it," I say, looking at him straight in the eye. "I've never been professionally involved with contemporary poetry."

"So? You have to be a professional?" he replies boldly. "You have all the qualifications to know whether it's poetry or not. Don't you have a Laurea degree in Letters, like me?"

"Yes, but it takes more than that to know if it's poetry." I pause to take a breath. "You have to know what to compare it to, what's being written nowadays; you have to have the broad picture. I just wanted to warn you."

"Oh, you're so difficult!" He laughs, closing the drawer. "You talk about judgment as if it were universal. You're not going to decide for posterity!" He brings his bad leg closer to the desk and thrusts the packet at me. "I just want to know what you think. I want to know if my poems say something to you. A long time ago I asked some experts whether I should continue writing or give up. They never answered me, so I never quit. It'd be a little late now, don't you think?"

He's shifted into the local dialect. I envy him. It helps him transform life into a joke. It helps connect an individual to a community. It removes the burden from him and transfers it to me.

"Now don't get all flustered," he adds. "I'm not asking you to make an investment, just a little effort."

"Why, sure!" I react with false vivacity. "I'd be pleased to do it. No trouble at all."

He raises his hand in front of his face as if to protect himself from being hit.

"Hold on. It doesn't end there."

I knew it. He's one of those people to whom you are always in debt.

"After you've read it," he says calmly, nodding toward the sheaf of poems in my hands, "and only after you're convinced"—he makes it seem like he's giving me a choice when actually he's taking one away—"then there's something else you can do for me."

"Sure," I say in resignation and with impudence. "What?"

"Can't you guess?"

I think about it quickly. Write a preface? No, I've never published anything. Make a selection of his poems? No, he's already done that. Pay an entry fee to some expensive prize? No, he's ruled those out.

"Your father-in-law. He's a lawyer, isn't he? He specializes in editorial contracts, doesn't he?" he asks calmly.

"How did you know?"

"I too have my sources," he says with a smile.

"Yes, but what can he do?"

"A lot," he says firmly. "He's in touch with the chief editors at the best publishing companies. A word from him is everything."

No autocrat ever had as much power as the one who ignores all limits.

"He doesn't have to say much. It's enough that he shows— how can I put it?—a special kind of interest. However," he says, raising his hand to make his point, "he really has to be interested. He has to believe in it. I don't want just a bland letter of recommendation."

He wants what they obtain.

"But you see"—I try to distance him—"my father-in-law doesn't know much about contemporary poetry either. He stopped at D'Annunzio."

"Not a bad place to stop," he says. "Anyway, for the rest, there's you."

"But there's another reason," I insist. "He doesn't have the power that you believe he has. He might be able to get you read, but he can't get you published."

"Now, slow down," he says patiently, as if he has to explain something to one of his students. "You've heard of the Mafia, haven't you?"

"Of course."

"Isn't the literary world a kind of Mafia?"

"Not all of it."

"A large part of it, though."

"A part, perhaps. But first you have to be involved in it. If you are, they know that if you receive something, you'll give something back and if you don't receive, then you'll get back at them." I'm quickly discovering a theory behind the Mafia that has never been clearer. "But my father-in-law isn't involved. They wouldn't even consider him."

"You mean they don't listen to him?"

"No, they listen to him but they're not afraid of him. That's the difference."

He follows what I'm saying with a bowed head, confused and let down. Surely he's weighing his alternatives. I know how arrogant and persevering those who oppose the system of recommendations can be, only to celebrate it under a different name.

He raises his head and looks at me. "You're saying he'd have a problem with a small book of poems?"

I have to stop him now or heavier threats will follow. "Perhaps someone else in his position would do it," I say, "but not him."

"He's an upright kind of guy."

"That's right."

"One of those men who breaks into a thousand pieces if you so much as touch him."

I laugh. "He's old-fashioned," I explain. "He stays within his territory, where he has authority."

"Authority! Now there's a strong word!" he exclaims. "Who do you think has authority in the world of poetry?"

"I don't know. A critic, maybe? An expert?"

He looks at me challengingly. "You don't, though. You're just a teacher. You never studied poetry."

We're getting to the point I feared, where irony turns into bitterness. "You're right," I say with a weak smile. "I'm not an expert. And especially not in your eyes."

"Why? 'No man is a prophet in his own country'?"

"That too," I say, letting myself be comforted by the quotation, which I usually find a consolation both in real situations and imaginary ones.

"But really, how do you consider yourself?" he insists.

"As one who earns too little for what he does."

"Is that all?"

"Yes," I reply. "If you're interested in culture but can't earn a living from it, you've got to be a little crazy. At the very most, you gain respect. On the other hand, if you earn well from it, it's all about career."

"It's all about money," he exclaims brightly. I can't tell whether he approves or disapproves. "Nothing else matters."

He's silent for a minute. He's thinking. He can't be happy about the turn in our conversation.

"Still!" he exclaims with cruel vivacity. "He wouldn't say no to a favor, not with all the bad luck you've had."

"He's been affected by it too," I reply, pretending not to have noticed the brutal way he spoke. We mentally correct other people's comments in order for the dialogue to continue. "Actually, he considers me partially responsible."

"Why?" he asks incredulously.

"You're always involved in what happens to you, at least somehow," I reply. "Especially if it's at someone else's expense."

It's true, but I'm exaggerating. And he notices.

"Are you sure about that?" he asks.

"I think I know him well enough," I say, trying to undermine him.

"I think I'm getting to know you," he says ominously. "And I can't tell if you're acting or if you're really like that."

"Really like what?"

"So cautious. You move so carefully!" With his hands he mimes the movements of a very slow animal, a bear or a sloth. "You'll never get anything done like that," he continues. "You have to make things happen in life!"

"I agree."

"You have to throw yourself at things," he repeats. "If you don't take risks you'll never learn your own limits."

"I think I know mine."

"Only too well!" he says. "You're overly scrupulous. You have too many doubts. If I were you, I wouldn't be here now."

"I can believe that," I reply.

I like my double-edged answers. They lend themselves to being interpreted in both ways, positive and negative, the positive one by the interlocutor and the negative one by me. But this time he picks up immediately on the negative one.

"Yes, but don't think it only affects me!" he goes on to say. "After all, we're in the same boat."

More than an assertion, it's a threat.

"And if the helmsman makes a mistake," he says testily, "he's not the only one who'll sink. You'll go down too."

"I see," I reply, even though I don't really understand where this boat's going.

"Do you understand what I'm saying?" he asks.

"Yes, but what exactly are you alluding to?"

"I'm alluding to us!" he says. "To your problem! Which has now become my own. Because I've chosen to take it on board."

"And I'm very grateful to you, I told you."

"Oh, yes, grateful," he murmurs, as if the adjective weren't enough. "You know how things happen in schools. I have to interpret the laws," he says, thumping his chest. "I have to do things that I don't have the right to do," he says, repeating the gesture.

"What exactly are you talking about?" I ask. A shiver runs through me.

"Limiting the number of students in the class! Otherwise Signorina Bauer will refuse to have a handicapped student in her classroom." He pauses, then adds, "I just don't know if I'll be able to manage it. I'm really not sure I can."

"Now, hold on just a minute," I say, and in my mind I'm thinking, *The bastard!* "You can't tell me this now!"

"Why not?" He raises his voice in indignation. "I am!"

"No. According to the law, you have to limit the number of students in the class." I try to speak calmly, but I feel my voice fading with the increasing anguish. "There's a law and you know it."

"Ultimately, it's up to the principal to interpret things on a case-by-case basis. I'm not sure that the administration will let me limit the size of the class."

It's getting hard for me to breathe.

"It's happened before and I didn't give up!" he adds, with malign triumph in his voice.

"Now listen carefully to me," I say, moving my chair closer to the desk. I'm trying to speak slowly but I realize I'm panting. "A handicapped student has the right to a smaller class size. I've done the research."

"Obviously not enough," he insists.

"If you don't limit the number of students so that it's acceptable to Signorina Bauer," I say, pointing my finger at him, my voice getting stronger, "just wait and see what will happen!"

I glare at him, seething with enmity.

"What are you trying to say?"

"Your school will be on the front pages of all the newspapers for not respecting the new laws. It'll be a scandal!"

In order to save an unreal situation and salvage what I can, I said "school," not him. He notices and is grateful for it, I can tell.

"Newspapers?" he asks. "You have clout with the newspapers?"

"My father-in-law! He'd do that for my son—and more!"

The mere thought of my father-in-law makes his face light up.

"Now don't get so worked up," he says slowly, looking at me.

"I was just making you aware of a possible problem. We're here to help each other, right?"

"Right," I say. There's nothing more I can say.

"You see, your father-in-law *can* make things happen. I'm sure of it. In this case as in publishing. That's why I chose to speak to you about my poems."

I have no strength left.

"You know, it really is vital to think about how one faces things. Suddenly, what was impossible is now possible. It's that way for my poems too, you'll see," he concludes.

I listen to him, drained, my legs weak with the prolonged tension. I can't put my child's future on the line for threats like these. In Italy one is never entirely sure of the law. There's always the risk that one will be overpowered by some higher authority.

"I'll see what I can do," I mumble, getting to my feet. The meeting is over. "But I can't promise anything. It doesn't depend on me."

"No," he replies, "it really *does* depend on you."

He stands up too, fiercely and vigorously, extending his stiff leg in my direction. He comes around to my side of the desk. Leaning heavily on his cane and lifting his bad leg slightly off the floor, he rests his hand on my shoulder.

"It's important that we get along; it doesn't take much."

I put his manuscript into my satchel.

"Keep me posted," he says. Then, in dialect, he says, "One hand washes the other, isn't that so? What do you say to that?"

"Goodbye," I say. We're at the door. "I'll see what I can do."

"Me too!" he exclaims, with laughing eyes. "And you know what I think? I think we're going to make it!"

I shake his hand. An uncomfortable solidarity has formed between us that pleases him.

"Do you want me to call the elevator for you?"

"No, I'll walk down."

"Lucky you!" he says. "I always have to take the elevator."

"Right," I say with a nod. "And if my son has to come upstairs, he'll have to take it too."

"We'll take it together!" he calls out, as I start down the stairs.

Pleasure Island

We take our seats on the folding chairs that have been arranged in a semicircle around the exercise mat on which she sits, cross-legged. She's wearing a black sweat suit that covers her long angular body. She glances at her Day-Glo wristwatch and smiles sarcastically as a woman with heavy makeup languidly enters the room in a cloud of perfume.

"We've been waiting for you," she says.

Without adjusting her pace, the latecomer makes her way over to the folding chairs and slowly takes a seat in the second row. Her son's case is not serious; he has trouble walking, and physiotherapy alone will probably take care of it. She tends to observe us with careful and detached curiosity, like a first-class traveler visiting the third-class deck. She never neglects to mention the minor nature of her son's condition. When we're discussing the most difficult cases she opens her eyes wide in a kind of theatrical solidarity, but you can tell that hearing other people's stories simply offers her yet another form of reassurance. She's not the only parent to react like that, just the most obvious and perhaps the stupidest. None of us are immune to it.

We're always glad to comfort those who are worse off and, in so doing, comfort ourselves. A classification of handicaps has become a silent object of competition between us. If we compete like this among ourselves, I suppose we shouldn't really be surprised at how others react.

"All right. Is everyone listening?" the doctor says, rising up to a crouching position, one hand on the mat in front of her.

"You'll have to talk about yourselves. That's right, about yourselves," she said solemnly at the first parents' meeting at the Center. And then she pointed at us, making us instantly feel guilty.

We have to get to the root of the problem. We need to talk about things sincerely, to use that infamous word; that's how she defined it. Her instructions are accompanied by shrill laughter, the kind she feels helps lessen the tension. How we experience the handicap, how the handicap has changed us, who we are now. Our experiences will be compared and gathered into a dossier by the Center. Eventually the material may even form the basis of a book.

"Are you pleased?" she asks.

A dark silence follows that finally unites us. We stare straight ahead, trying to avoid her gaze as she looks around the room in careful scrutiny. We've regressed back to schoolchildren; none of us dares look at the teacher while she decides which one of us to call on.

"We won't talk about what goes on here at the Center; it will be our Pleasure Island. I want you to talk about what goes on outside."

"Enough of this 'Pleasure Island'!" a heavy man says gruffly, his neck puffing out like a toad's, his eyes dilating, his cheeks turning purple. "Let's begin by doing away with the name!"

"Why, don't you like it, Signor Colnaghi?" the doctor asks calmly, rocking back on her heels and sticking out her chest proudly. "What don't you like about it?"

"The name: Pleasure Island," he replies. "What on earth does it have to do with us?"

"I agree," I hear myself saying. Why am I doing this? I'm not sure, but now I have to keep going. Signor Colnaghi turns toward me, overwhelmed with gratitude. "It's the wrong formula."

She looks at me with a shared sense of irony. "So you're against me now too, Signor Frigerio?" Then, after a pause she adds, "Of course we don't have to use that name. What do you think, Signora?" She turns to a diminutive lady sitting in the front row who keeps her hands folded over her knees in a gradually intensifying grip. I've noticed her before; she's one of those very shy people who, when called on to speak in public, would just love to disappear. The kind of person who dreams of saying memorable things and fears saying the ridiculous.

"It sounds fine to me," she replies weakly.

The doctor jumps to her feet. We know how proud she is of doing this. Her existence is based on passionately serving those who are devoid of such agility. She teases us with it. She's a good woman, we're reluctantly forced to admit.

She laughs brightly, the way she does at the best of times. "Signor Colnaghi and Signor Frigerio don't like Pleasure Island. What about the rest of you?"

The others hesitate; they shift uncomfortably on their chairs, torn between adulation and truth, tradition and secession.

"I get it. You don't like it either. So we'll do away with it. No more Pleasure Island from now on. But what about the Center. Are you pleased with the Center?"

Yes! The Center, yes, a liberated chorus of voices exclaims, but hidden in their voices lies a combination of sincerity and untruthfulness, conviction and perplexity. Just as in school, there's the same divided unanimity.

"We couldn't ask for better treatment," Signor Colnaghi says, dabbing at his forehead with a handkerchief, both proud and fearful of his unexpected triumph, "but Pleasure Island was a bit euphoric."

"Yes, Signor Colnaghi, I know. It's been discussed," she says patiently, lowering her gaze.

He wants to say more, as often happens when someone has already concluded. "We live it differently."

"I know." She nods. Then she looks up. "That's right. How do you live the experience of the Center?"

She's picked up where she left off. How do we live the experience of the Center?

We grow serious: focused, intense, almost troubled. The vacation on Pleasure Island is over.

Favors

The same person who'll refuse to do a favor for you if you ask in the evening might have been willing to do it had you asked earlier in the day. It all depends on someone's mood. There's no way of knowing for sure. These are the hypothetical certainties that are sources of joy when we are tempestuous and of distress when we are not.

That's why I can't risk making a mistake with my father-in-law. What's the best time to ask him a favor?

"What kind of favor?" Franca asks.

"Publishing."

"Never," she says.

"Good," I reply, encouraged by our matrimonial exchange.

"Who's it for?"

"The guy with the limp."

With some distress I realize I have brutally used the principal's disability against him. It doesn't usually happen to people who are either directly or indirectly affected by a handicap. If someone uses the abusive epithets "spastic" or "mongoloid," you can be sure that no one in their family is either of those.

Misfortunes have varying kinds of effects on us, linguistic ones being the most immediate. We become sensitive to the vocabulary associated with the problem. We could even say, by way of inference, that writers are perennially sensitive to the misfortunes of language, even if they're never affected by them. Nor do they expect to be, in order to reflect on the variations in meaning. This helps explain why the language of the handicapped has become a victim of neuroses. People wonder why "blind" has become *vision-impaired* and "deaf" is *hearing-impaired*. One plausible explanation could be that "blind" irreparably defines a person, while "vision-impaired" circumscribes the absence of a function.

The antithesis of this is furnished by the example of the limping principal. The most circumspect definition for him, according to the current language of the handicapped, would be to say he has problems walking, in the same way the mother of a child who stutters would say her child has problems speaking. Another way of defining the principal, one that is elegantly cloaked in the formal language of culture, would be to say that he is *claudicate*. But "claudicate principal" reveals an all-too-obvious irony.

The limping principal is a bitter, obstinate, and hostile man. His presence suggests both an authoritarian figure weakened by a physical defect and a devil—as in the novels of Lesage—perched high above the roofs of Madrid, the same image I was trying to suggest earlier. This confirms two things: that debility is a treacherous card to be played at just the right moment and that solidarity is not the most common attribute among those suffering from handicaps.

.   .   .

Perhaps the best moment to ask the favor is when he comes back from his car ride with Paolo. He's always nervous before leaving, as if he were preparing for a sortie against the enemy. He straps Paolo so tightly into his seat that the boy sits up stiffly; not even his head lolls forward. He still hasn't gotten used to Paolo's anomalies. His face lights up when someone doesn't immediately notice Paolo's "problems," as if this reassures him of a future normality. "He'll never be normal," I once told him in exasperation. We can put up with our own mistakes but not when we see them replicated in others. "That's what you think!" he had replied, adding, "Nature performs miracles!"

He never assisted in Paolo's physical therapy. Franca managed to involve friends, relatives, neighbors, and peers in turning his head and stretching his limbs, but she never dared ask her father. Or, rather, she limited herself to asking him once, recalling a Sicilian proverb that says when a friend doesn't hear you the first time, it means he doesn't want there to be a second time.

Perhaps it seemed unnatural to him that a child should be as frail as an elderly person. It must have seemed like physiological subversion, even though I explained to him that, in fact, physiology anticipates such a subversion. If it didn't, Paolo would never have been able to put alternate circuits into function, as the neurologists had predicted he would.

"Why do you think Paolo survived?" I asked him once.

"Because he's strong!" he answered, with a humble jolt of pride.

"No, because he's weak," I said. "He gains strength from his flexibility."

"Enough of your talk!" he'd replied. "I just don't follow you."

Paolo offered him the most extreme opportunity to reexamine his beliefs, but that was the last thing he wanted to do. Dominated by hierarchical ideas on nature and society, he was forced to contend with his grandson's condition, which posed insoluble problems to his understanding of the meaning of life. Contrary to what one would generally believe, diversity makes us feel diverse and we do not easily forgive that. My father-in-law died believing his grandson was diverse in appearance only. That was his most tenacious hope; the fear of being proved otherwise rendered him fanatical. Jung wrote that fanaticism is an overcompensated doubt, but my father-in-law never even managed to begin compensating for his.

He once told me that as a young man he and his friends would wait in the cinema for homosexual men to give themselves away so they could ambush them and teach them a lesson or two. It struck me that he had used the word *lesson*. It certainly had taught a lot to the person being attacked but nothing at all to the aggressor. Fifty years later, the lesson continues to elude him.

I wait for him to return from his outing with Paolo.

The green car enters the courtyard of the building with its lights on. It's only late afternoon, but he turns on his lights at the same time the municipality turns on the streetlights. It's one of the many rituals he celebrates with maniacal observation and of which he is especially proud, as if it were some kind of merit. Another one he's proud of is his perfect attendance at a club to which he belongs. "I've never been absent," he once told me proudly. "Never!" He reminded me of an admiral who, after saving his crew and passengers, had fearlessly gone down with his ship, the only difference being that my father-in-law lived to tell the story.

He opens his door slowly and walks around the rear of the car to open Paolo's door. In the meantime I've gotten Paolo's go-cart out of the garage and wheeled it over. He unfastens Paolo's seat belt, picks him up, and lowers him into the go-cart with graceful ease. I know that this maneuver, done with delicate precision, fills him with the silent joy of an artisan in front of work well done.

"I've been meaning to ask you a favor," I begin, as Paolo pedals off in zigzags across the courtyard.

"Tell me," he replies.

"I know it runs counter to your moral and ethical code."

"Get to the point," he says.

"The principal of the school that Paolo will attend is disabled."

"Him too!" He throws his hands up in the air.

"Yes, and he'd like to publish a book of his poems with an imprint of your caliber."

He's sensitive to this wrong word, but it puts him in a good mood, alluding to a power he doesn't have.

"How do I fit in?" he asks.

I know he wants to hear the favor that is being asked of him in clear and precise terms. It's a practice I used to associate with men of a certain age, until I understood that these men of a certain age have accumulated a certain amount of experience over the years and they're not wrong to expect it. They're tired of doing favors for people who make it seem as though they themselves are actually doing the favor.

"He'd like you to talk to an important editor about his work. He thinks you can do anything."

"It's not true, but I can do it this time," he says. "I did quite an important favor for one recently. Give me the manuscript."

He nods slyly and says no more.

I am dumbfounded.

"I suppose you want to read it first before giving it to him," I add, already responding to this situation for which I was unprepared.

"Why on earth would I do that? Give it to me now, and I'll talk to him about it later this week. Did you like it?"

"Yes," I say, taken aback. "It's not bad."

"Only 'not bad'?" he says, smiling. "I was hoping for better."

"Actually, for me, not bad means pretty good."

"What's 'pretty good'?" he rebuts. "Give it to me and say no more!" He points to the car. "Would you mind backing it out while I go and say goodbye to Paolo?"

"Not at all," I reply, opening the door and climbing in.

Everything feels easy, light, simple. I look up. In the square of sky between the buildings, I can see the first stars.

I back up quickly. My father-in-law shrinks at the far end of the courtyard. For some reason, I have always imagined him in breeches. But he's never worn them.

Miss Bauer

Her name is Elisa Bauer. She's from Bolzano and she's thirty-two years old. She has never had a disabled child in her class and seems, when we meet her, visibly concerned about the prospect of having one. She wanted to meet us; we live about three hundred yards away from the school.

Her blond hair is gathered in a bun at the nape of her neck. She moves with ease and elegance and is as attractive as she is reserved, more athletic than sensual. She's pretty but her focus is uneven. She can seem cold, typical of women who are afraid of showing their emotions.

While we take turns telling her about our child, she keeps her eyes downcast. We've become experts at describing him in the most charming terms. We smile cheerfully. But it's the wrong strategy. I fear she's starting to think that our child is a monster. She asked what he suffered from and the answer—dystonic spastic quadriparesis—left her stunned.

I close my eyes for a moment while Franca clarifies some of Paolo's difficulties. We always make the mistake of trying to minimize them, even with doctors. Especially with doctors. We try not to tire him out before his appointments. We tell him to be that which we lack most: calm. We get upset each time he makes a mistake and then he makes more mistakes than usual, as if wanting to justify our panic. I'm afraid we're a monstrous couple, overwrought with fear and united only in the absurd hope of overcoming it. If anything, we should present him in the worst light possible, so as to avoid a comfortable diagnosis and obtain a more plausible one.

When the doctors become aware of our circumlocutions, they react with poorly concealed impatience. We go to great lengths to try to show them that our child is more normal than they might believe. The truth is never quite so elusive and distressing as in those moments.

The mute resistance of Miss Bauer is suffocating me. So without turning to look at Franca, who sits on my right, even though I can imagine what her reaction will be, I speak up.

"You have a difficult task ahead of you. We know how hard it can be. You will have to devote yourself to it entirely. At times you might even regret having wanted him in your class."

I don't really believe what I'm saying, but when she looks up at me her gaze is calm.

"Now don't exaggerate," Franca says. I squeeze her arm until it hurts and we stare at each other with reciprocal rage.

"That sounds like a constructive approach. That's what I wanted to hear," Miss Bauer says, without noticing a thing. She looks down again.

Franca rubs her arm. I know what waits for me later. So does she. We both know. Maybe that's what marriage is all about.

"I'd rather be prepared for the worst, not for the best," Miss Bauer adds.

"How right you are!" I exclaim, as if discovering this as a newly minted truth.

Miss Bauer looks up; her eyes are misty with emotion. "That's the way I am. So far it's been a strong point in my work. Don't you think it's a good thing?"

"Definitely!" I say, with the prodigal enthusiasm that we have when it doesn't cost anything. It's what differentiates visitors to an artist's studio from buyers.

Bit by bit, as she speaks, she loses her charm. She's reasonable, focused, and enthusiastic. I'm relieved for Paolo but a little concerned for her. It's as if, in a game of chess, the player with the advantage were suddenly to surrender. I wonder whether she'd be upset by this comparison. She'd probably be more upset with me.

"Look at Paolo's photographs," Franca says, getting up from the sofa and taking down one of the frames in the hallway in which she's collected some of his most successful pictures. She's incorrigible, and yet she obtains what she wants, even if she does go further than I would. In any case, I've noticed that the legitimacy of the goal, however difficult, makes one ethically cynical.

Miss Bauer is looking at me with a knowing smile, as if she knows she can count on me to help her resist kindness. Franca talks about Paolo. She makes him out to be a communicative and easygoing person. By the end Miss Bauer is laughing at the story of how, when someone asks Paolo on the intercom, "Is that you?" he replies from the lobby, "No!"

"He takes advantage of the linguistic tools available to him," I comment. "Like in *arte povera*."

She shows her appreciation for the linguistic reference with a professional nod. Franca feels momentarily excluded but then picks up again.

"Don't mind him! He only pays attention to language," she says with a laugh. "So much is communicated without words."

Miss Bauer smiles. I smile too. It will take me at least twenty years to figure out that Franca is right.

Our conversation gets interrupted. Franca has gone to make sure that Paolo's room is tidy before showing it.

Miss Bauer takes a sip of orange soda from her yellow glass. The whole apartment is brightly colored. The physiotherapist recommended strong colors for Paolo's room but gradually Franca has extended the color scheme to the whole apartment. Sofas, armchairs, dining chairs, closets, blocks, balls, and toys— all are brightly colored. Together they form what looks like the background for a cartoon. I've noticed this unreal and festive quality in the homes of other families with similar problems (though no two cases are alike, both within and outside of the norm). Space is given over to childhood with a freedom that childhood itself doesn't know, so used to making do with whatever bits of the serious adult world it can obtain. It's a sad reversal: order makes itself felt in artificial disorder; the pleasure of games vanishes with the awareness of their function.

"Would you like to see Paolo's room?" Franca says from the doorway.

Miss Bauer places her drink on the glass table. "Your wife is absolutely wonderful," she says with a smile, getting to her feet.

"I know." I nod. "But it shouldn't have happened to her."

"Why her in particular?" she asks. "It shouldn't happen to anyone."

"She's been wounded in the place where she is the weakest."

"Or perhaps the strongest," Miss Bauer comments.

I can hear them talking. It's too bad she came to visit while Paolo isn't here, but when she called Paolo had already left with my father-in-law for a drive. But maybe it's better this way: Miss Bauer is taking careful inventory of his difficulties. She's convinced that only by distributing them evenly across time will she be able to overcome them.

I'm beginning to feel more certain that she'll be the right teacher for him: She actually seems only reluctantly enthusiastic, a trait she must have learned the hard way, but at the same time she's a stranger to discouragement, which is a no-less-frightening adversary.

Once I never would have used the adjective "right." It seems to neutralize all efforts of the common aspiration to perfection. Now, instead, I've adopted the protective language of the majority, much in the same way that surrendering to the use of medical jargon in the hospital allows you to join the anonymous ranks of the sick and, in turn, affirms your dependence on an authority figure for assistance. Even handicaps are defined by words that placate an immediate anxiety, that of knowing what it is. The next phase is discovering that the definition doesn't really define it. Still, a step has been taken in the right direction.

It's getting dark. I stand at the living room window and look out at the rooftops and skyscrapers and the brightly lit streets. The same landscape that on other occasions fills me with disquiet now gives me a sense of intimacy. Another obstacle has been overcome.

Miss Bauer comes out of Paolo's room. She looks radiant; her cheeks are bright from conversation.

"I have to run," she says.

Maybe I'm too attentive to words, like Franca says, but *run* is a verb that bothers me right now, even if she is right to want to escape that crowded room, its joyless toys, optimistic despair, and anguished hopes.

"I'm glad you came to see us."

"It was my duty," she says, suddenly growing serious.

She's worried that we'll exchange it for a favor. It occurs to me that many people make their duties pass as favors. Real schools are made of exceptions, and they're as rare as apologetic teachers.

"I'll accompany you," I say.

We ride down in the brightly lit elevator. She stands in the corner.

"How long have you been teaching here?" I ask.

"Six years."

"Do you like it?"

"Yes, except for the principal, at first."

She stops herself. She's already said too much.

"Meaning?"

"He was a little insistent."

She offers no more.

"Where did you teach before?"

"In Bolzano, for three years."

"Why did you leave Bolzano?"

She hesitates for a moment.

"Because of a person. Bad judgment," she says.

I nod as if I knew who she was talking about.

"The wrong person," she adds.

Perhaps I too am a wrong person. We never stop discovering that others are the wrong people in the belief that we can extricate ourselves from a common destiny. But it's never a good idea to delve into these details with our closest relatives; we are always badly surprised.

"Are you over it?" I ask.

"Yes, but only recently."

She's not over it yet.

"It must have been very important for you."

Important is an adjective that people like because it makes something seem important per se when actually it's important only for them.

"Yes," she answers quickly. "Teaching saved me."

So there's the road to salvation, I think. Ultimately, her misadventures will be important for Paolo too.

"What a delusion," she adds.

"I bet," I reply.

Vague images run through my mind of contemporary stories, as well as of stories that happened hundreds of years ago. Miss Bauer runs a hand through her hair as if she wants to distance a thought.

"Do you help your wife?" she asks.

"At times, yes," I reply, looking down.

"What do you mean, 'at times'?"

We're on the ground floor. I open the elevator door for her, and she steps out into the unlit lobby.

"Sometimes I'm absent," I add.

"Physically, you mean?"

"Physically and mentally."

"And you say so without remorse?" she asks, turning to look at me.

"No, I say it with remorse."

"Why don't you do something about it?"

We go down the three steps toward the front door.

"I suppose because I'm egocentric," I reply, opening the

glass door for her. I know it's too simple an answer. To admit one's errors is the first alibi for repeating them.

In fact, Miss Bauer doesn't let herself be distracted. "Maybe there's some other reason?"

I get the clear feeling that I am being put on trial. Who gives her the right? Me, probably. There's nothing like feeling guilty for having someone attribute it to you.

"It's a question of strong points," I reply. "I, for example, would be a terrible teacher for Paolo."

"Really?" she asks incredulously.

Miss Bauer is becoming incredibly oppressive. She's avenging herself on me for the wrongs that she has suffered.

"Yes, I've tried. I become aggressive, nervous, and impatient."

"Couldn't you change?"

"You can't. Or rather, you can but the other person suffers as a consequence. The results are negative for both of us."

We're walking down the sidewalk. It's a warm evening.

"Which way are you going, Miss Bauer?"

"To the subway station." After a few steps, she turns to me and asks, "So what are some of your strong points?"

"I didn't mean it that way," I say with a smile.

It's odd to find myself at sunset on the crowded sidewalks of Corso Buenos Aires defending myself to my son's teacher.

"What did you mean then?" she asks, without letting up.

"That I only do a portion of what I could do. I know the alternative would be a failure."

"And your wife?"

"She does practically everything."

I avoid looking at her so I don't have to see her triumphant smile. I know about female solidarity and how it has the not-insignificant advantage of reason. That's why I usually cling to the remnants.

"And she doesn't ask you to do more?"

"No. It would just make things worse."

Miss Bauer attracts indiscreet glances; people turn to look at her. She defends herself with a show of indifference, typical of someone who sets too much store by this sort of thing.

"Your wife is happy."

It's impossible to tell whether it's a question or a reluctant affirmation.

"No. But you see, that's not the point." It's getting hard to speak; I'm discovering what I think. "The point is that we are always at our extreme limits. If I carve out spaces for myself—we can even call them privileges—I can manage to hold up—"

"Otherwise you'd run away from it all," she interrupts. "Is that what you want to say?" She doesn't even give me time to answer. "Many men would act the same way in similar situations."

"Why do you think so poorly of me?" I ask.

"I don't think poorly of you."

"You mustn't forget about the institution that doubles our neuroses."

"And what would that be?"

"Marriage, Miss Bauer. And don't laugh."

There, I got her. I feel better now.

"I didn't think you had those kind of feelings about marriage," she says.

"Sure you did!" I exclaim. "Otherwise you wouldn't have piled up so many accusations against me."

"They're not accusations," she says, reacting in the way that she, Miss Bauer, knows she has to react. "They're questions so I can understand how the work with Paolo gets distributed."

"Unevenly," I reply. "That's the truth. I'm not happy about it, but that's the way it is."

I've reacquired a resigned pride in my wrongdoings. She has moderated her tone. As long as she was judging me she felt invulnerable. But to be judged as an accuser has made her slightly more cautious.

"It's a very complicated situation," I go on to say. "Very hard. Luckily, I don't think Paolo has suffered because of it. However, if you feel the need, you can talk to me about it any time."

"Fine," she says, stopping at the stairwell that leads down to the subway. Her cheeks are bright and there is a soft expression in her eyes.

I reach out and shake her hand, pausing to squeeze it for a moment.

"I think we can use the *tu* form," I say. And then with vertiginous perception, but late, almost comically, I add, "Between colleagues."

"We'll see," she replies.

She's become Miss Bauer again.

She starts to go down the stairs, then turns to wave goodbye. From where I stand on the sidewalk I watch her disappear into the darkness.

A rosy light radiates over Corso Buenos Aires, illuminating the faces of passersby as they emerge from the shadows.

I turn toward home. My mind is confused. I am tired and stunned. It's as if I had been fighting, first for Paolo and then for myself.

Paolo's cause has been won, at least for now. But what about mine? I tried to persuade Miss Bauer, but who was I really trying to convince? Now, on this glowing evening, I am tearfully certain that I'll never succeed.

The Go-Cart

He goes to school by go-cart. The go-cart was one of Franca's ideas.

I used to take him to the park in his stroller. He would sit on a bench by the fountain and watch the ice-cream vendors and the balloon salesmen, the children rolling on the grass and the joggers on the crunching gravel, always the same panorama. Only now can I imagine the torture. Back then I just couldn't bring myself to think about it. I was too worried: about my own personal survival and—without surrendering to the moralistic complacency of self-abnegation—my family's. I was forced to be cruelly selective in how I distributed my energies (at least that was my alibi at the time). In that luminous festive park landscape, though, the pedal-powered go-carts always caught Paolo's eye. The children behind the wheel were exultant; they cruised between people and crossed easily over the paths. You could rent them from the parking attendant under the plane trees, near the entrance to the Planetarium. At first the man wouldn't tell us where he had bought them, fearing who knows what kind of competition. Fearful people see danger in everything; they practically invent dangers in order to intensify the pleasure of avoiding them. All in vain, too, because fear is born on the inside, like the insatiable thirst of a person suffering from dropsy.

When questioned by my father-in-law, however, the coarse repugnant man revealed the name of the mechanic who repaired the go-carts for him. From there it was easy to trace the factory where they were made.

When Alfredo saw the shiny red go-cart with its sculpted rubber racing wheels in the courtyard of our building he couldn't hide his intolerance. For two consecutive Christmases, when he was six and seven, he had asked for one. Now he was too big. He couldn't fit into it. When his mother saw him trying to squeeze into it from the balcony, she scolded him, telling him he was too old for such things now. He probably suffered because of it, as if we had confiscated a childhood he had not been able to enjoy. Once I even saw him kick the tires; I smacked the back of his neck in the very same place my father had smacked me when I had knocked over a fishbowl. Then, when he started crying miserably, I observed how we repeat on our own children the very same acts of violence we ourselves were subjected to, albeit unwillingly. (How the unconscious assists us!) Criminology texts talk about such things, but Renaissance documents on the family do not.

Paolo, on the other hand, could easily be lowered into the go-cart from above, but at first he could barely make it move. To push one foot and then the other in alternation did not come instinctively to him; it was a conquest. From the window of our apartment I'd watch him in the courtyard below, lurching forward with irregular movements. At times I'd curse at life in a whisper, even if there was no one around to hear me.

Sometimes Paolo would rest his forehead against the steering wheel. I couldn't tell if he was overwhelmed by a sense of powerlessness or by fatigue. I remember a young physiotherapist who once compared the reaction of a disabled child faced by a flight of stairs to that of an elderly person. "Now do you understand what they feel?" she'd ask. We nodded our heads, but an elderly person's experience of stairs was just as foreign to us as that of a disabled child. Only by verifying the effect of time on our own bodies does the pain become comprehensible and the foreignness familiar. Everyone knows we grow old—but, as Trotsky said, old age is the most unpredictable event that happens after the age of forty-five. From a theoretician of the permanent revolution, this confession should not be undervalued.

The young physiotherapist gave us other examples having to do with muscles and fatigue. She had an extremely flexible associative capacity, which was at times disconcerting and confusing. We'd make the wrong connection and understand even less, distracted by images that didn't make sense. At other times—gesticulating with powerful mimicry and speaking with unexpected enthusiasm—she'd help us understand the particular problems of a handicap as well as situations on which the handicap had an indirect effect. Finally, we understood that everything has an indirect relationship to handicaps. When we say that such-and-such an experience helps us understand the experience of the handicapped, we omit the most important part: Dealing with the handicap helps us understand ourselves.

She told us, for example, how similar some muscular exercises are to the various phases of the Tour de France. The cyclists who ride day after day don't "see" the mountains ahead of them. If they could "see" that, cumulatively, they rise higher than Mount Everest, they'd give up trying to break records and they'd always be looking back to see what they had accomplished. Overattentiveness to a partial goal induces us not to think about the final one, keeping us, in many cases, from ever reaching it.

Paolo transformed the go-cart into an anomalous car; it became a mechanical projection of himself. While Franca observed that he improved each time, I'd observe that he was making too little progress. But mine was less an observation than a fear. (How frequently we substitute fears for observations!) After three months of practice, Paolo was zipping around the courtyard, turning the wheel boldly to avoid crashing into the columns. He must have particularly loved that maneuver, because I watched him do it over and over, each time getting a little closer to the obstacle. Then he learned how to go backward. He experimented with slamming into things, practically knocking himself out of the seat. After four months, he was ready to go beyond the courtyard.

He careened down sidewalks and zigzagged between people. Some of them smiled and stepped aside so he could pass; others would turn around, frowning hesitantly, to verify if what they had seen was actually so.

He'd enter the schoolyard through a side gate. There was a small hill. He had to pedal hard to make it to the top. Then, triumphantly, he'd lift his feet off the pedals and let the go-cart cruise down the other side, until he stepped on the pedals again and either skidded out of control or came to a complete stop. Franca, who'd follow him on foot, would scold him each time in the same complicit way. There's something reassuring and ritualistic about familial scolding: the certainty of continuity through disapproval.

The go-cart was a luminous presence in Paolo's boyhood. During the day, the janitor kept it locked in a closet under a stairwell. The envy of all the other children, it helped transform his inferiority into a superiority. It was a temporary sensation, but no more illusory than many others we consider long-lasting.

Today I saw the go-cart in the storage area in the basement, and it had an altogether different effect on me. I was walking across the dusty room in the dark, paying attention to the uneven cement floor, when I saw it in a corner, illuminated by a diagonal shaft of light that came from a slit in the ceiling. It was covered in a veil of spiderwebs. It looked rusty, dirty, and useless. It looked like a fossilized skeleton. I was scared to touch it, as if it were the ruin of a dream.

Is a Child More Important than an Airplane?

"Don't you ever make mistakes when you write?" the doctor asks me, part in jest and part complicitly.

"Yes," I say, "but it's not the same thing."

"I see," he says, looking sarcastically at the audience gathered in the assembly room of the Center. "It's never the same thing. Mistakes are what other people do."

He's in a difficult situation, and he's doing everything he can to make it worse for himself. I understand men like that. They are both incited and excited by the hostility they arouse in others and their own natural antipathy. They paint the most narrow-minded picture of themselves and then unfortunately live up to it. But they're not the worst.

This pediatrician is visiting the Center because he accepted an invitation to hear out those parents who wanted to voice their complaints about the medical assistance they received before, during, and after their children's births. That takes courage.

These stories are hard; they're recriminations that have been exacerbated by time, by those long periods that despair reserves for reflection. Joy is volatile; its only concern is not to dissolve.

But the kind of pain that cannot place blame on destiny, the kind that has carelessness and the cynicism of man to blame, is relentless.

"We're not here to prosecute anyone," the doctor, Director of the Center, begins by saying. "We're here tonight to discuss to what extent the medical profession is responsible for handicaps—even if, statistically speaking, the situation tonight is somewhat unfair, as our public is made up entirely of those who have not been favored by chance."

She laughs quickly. It sounds like a gasp. It echoes emptily in the silent room. Typical. She wants to express solidarity with the parents and yet defend the medical ranks, for whom she spares no sarcasm.

"I'm ready to be lynched," says the guest pediatrician, with a smile that no one returns.

And so we hear stories about diagnoses that were carelessly made in the heat of the moment in the belief that they would be hidden behind an alibi of ethics. Instead, they smothered any such ethics: "It would be better for your son if you considered an institute." We hear stories about diagnoses pronounced with irresponsible optimism, in hopes of distracting attention from the present torment: "Don't worry, time will heal everything." We hear accounts of pediatricians with no concept of infantile neurology; we hear accounts of clinicians who know nothing about rehabilitative therapy.

"It's not just that the doctors are poorly prepared," Signor Colnaghi says, in his deep voice. "Basically, they're incompetent."

"What's the difference?" the pediatrician asks, with exaggerated amazement.

"The difference is that if a doctor knows his limits he'll turn to a specialist," Signor Colnaghi says, looking for consent toward the Director. "But if he doesn't, he'll attempt to form his own diagnosis. Do you have any idea what the consequences are?"

The Director joins in. "Children come to us when they're four and five years old. By then we've lost precious time. A specialist would have known what to do."

The pediatrician listens with professional impassivity.

"What do you think, Professor Frigerio?" she asks, looking over at me. "Do you think it's a cultural issue?"

"I suppose I would have to say so, yes," I reply. I feel like a student who's been called on to validate what the professor has just said. It's an embarrassing script, especially for the guest. We're always called on to recite a part that's not our own. "I think that culture is an indicator of what we do not know."

Without wanting to, I have become a little Socrates. (It happens when we speak in public.) I look desperately for a way out:

"A doctor has to be prudent; he can't afford to make a mistake. It's better to ask for another person's help. It's all right not to know something. A doctor can't put a person's life at risk."

"And so we're back to what we were talking about before," says the pediatrician, folding his arms across his chest. "Don't you ever make mistakes?"

"But I have a different kind of job!" I say heatedly. "If I put a comma in the wrong place, only one out of ten people will notice and nothing will come of it. But if you make a mistake with a child, he'll end up with brain damage. I'm not a doctor. I'm not even an airplane pilot."

"An airplane pilot?" the pediatrician asks caustically.

"An airplane pilot can't be distracted, especially when he's landing, or neither he nor his passengers will survive."

"So you're comparing a child to an airplane."

"No, I'm comparing the doctor to the pilot," I say. My heart rate has gone up, my veins are pulsing. Evidently, for him, a child is less important than an airplane. "What made you want to be a doctor? The man who helps a child to be born is flying an airplane."

The doctor looks down; he has perceived my emotions. He understands that it is not the right moment to contradict me. This is how many problems get resolved.

I try to control myself. "A child is more important than an airplane."

"I agree," he says patiently, but with a look of sincere puzzlement on his face.

Balancing Lessons

Halfway down the hall I suddenly let go. He doesn't fall. He wavers unsteadily, his rubber-soled shoes seemingly stuck to the rug. He reaches out for the wall with his right hand to catch himself but drops to his knees anyway. He then quickly looks up at me as I lift my gaze from my wristwatch.

"Twelve seconds!" I say. "Well done, Paolo. Now let's try again."

When I help him to his feet he lets his whole body go, as if drained. It looks horrible, but he does it to save his strength. I understand this only later. There are so many things we come to understand only later. The weak, on the other hand, lucid in the vast wealth of their resources, understand right away.

He's standing up again. I let go for a second but he falls backward. His eyes glaze over as if he has been hit by something. I manage to grab his arm. His inert weight makes him do a half twirl before slamming into the wall and sliding to the ground like a marionette. He's slow at using his arms to block his fall. He's slow at acquiring through reflection those movements that the so-called reflexes provide without thinking. He lost all bodily knowledge and has to relearn it consciously. Millions of years condensed into a decade: he has to simulate naturalness, imitate swiftness, and fake alacrity. This is his second birth—and it's into a world in which even we are becoming disabled.

"Would you please stop making the child fall?" Franca calls out from down the hall.

Parents' Meeting

One of the parents—a smug chubby woman, a math teacher by profession—poses a problem to the group. She gestures delicately with her hands. You can tell she likes to hear herself speak; that's why she says she wants to hear what we have to say. It works every time.

I have decided to simplify her polished language, which overflows with syntactical affectations and refined parenthetical clauses, illuminated by a noun—*idiolect*—thrown in with weighty nonchalance. To simplify (and declare as much) is one of the despotic and comforting privileges of the omniscient narrator, a figure who has been despised both in the past as well as by me (they actually know so very little).

The problem is this: her thirteen-year-old son, who has an attention deficit disorder, as the person next to me callously but succinctly explains, can't keep up with her when she tutors him in math, and she grows impatient with him.

"What do you do?" the doctor asks. I can see she's growing impatient, too.

"I slap him, but then I feel worse than he does."

How typically egocentric, I think to myself, to take pride in guilt as well as in merit.

"It's not enough to feel bad," the doctor scolds her. "You just can't do that!"

"I know," she says contritely. "That's why I wanted your opinion. I don't know why I do it."

I've always been afraid of math teachers, even when they indulged me, even when they went back over things I never would have understood on my own and explained them from the beginning, calmly and clearly. Actually, it was at those times above all that I felt I was being suffocated by panic because my sense of guilt would increase. Their knowledge was like a form of highly disciplined and extremely logical terrorism.

"Interrupt your lesson," the doctor suggests calmly. "Go and get something to drink. Distract yourself. You just cannot do that to your child!"

"I know," she replies, simulating uncontrollable anxiety. "But what I'd really like to know"—she's knitting her fingers together—"is why I react like that. Where does it come from? Intuitively, I think I know, but I'd like confirmation."

Another thing: They always know the answer. They only want an audience to hear them out.

"It's love-hate, don't you think?" she says, almost begging. "That's what we feel for our children. We love them too much."

Like many mothers who don't really feel it, she fakes an epic sense of maternity. The words of an American pedagogue come to mind: "If you want to do more for your children, do less."

The embarrassed parents listen in silence. At times, the blackmail of language prevents us from showing the repugnance it triggers in us.

The doctor looks to me for assistance. "Professor Frigerio, what do you think about this? You're a teacher too; surely you've tutored your son—"

"No, actually I rarely tutor him," I reply, "because it has the same effect on me."

"Do you slap your son too?" the doctor asks sarcastically.

"No, but there are worse offenses. A degrading look hurts. Intolerance is just as bad."

The math teacher sticks out her chest; she's pleased to have found someone whom she sees as an ally. "And it happens with our own children, the ones we love most. It doesn't happen with other students, the ones who pay to be tutored."

"That's the whole point," I say gravely.

"What is?"

"To begin with, the lesson you're giving your son is atypical. You're not getting paid for it."

The math teacher looks at me in amazement.

"That's the first frustrating thing about it," I say, "and it can't be ignored."

"What a cynic you are!" the math teacher exclaims.

"I'm not the problem," I say. "The problem is the lesson. A free lesson has to be gratifying in other ways. But because the student in this case just doesn't understand, the lesson fosters new frustrations."

I am pleased with the level of calm I am maintaining.

"Then, added to these frustrations," I go on to say, "is an even greater delusion: that the student is our child."

"The love-hate relationship I was talking about before," the teacher suggests.

"No," I reply, looking down. "I wouldn't call it that. I would call it hate. You, in that precise moment, hate your son. That's all. It's pure hate."

"What on earth are you saying?"

She has turned imploringly toward the doctor, but the doctor does not volunteer a word.

"You don't have to explain," I say. "You're hurting him. You'll love him later. In that particular moment, though, you hate him."

She looks back toward the doctor.

"What do you think? Is it true that I feel this way?"

"Why ask me?" she says. "They're your feelings."

Sea Rescue

I'm sitting with the doctor in her glass-walled office. The appointments are over for the day, the lights have been turned off in the therapy room, the physiotherapists are getting dressed to go home, and she's smoking a briar pipe that's as long and narrow as her face. I'm telling her what happened last August in Fano.

A friend of mine from Ancona comes to visit. Our two families decide to go to the beach. It's like a scene out of a nineteenth-century novel. A strong wind is blowing along the coast. Ominous dark waves crash against the stone jetties that enclose the small bay. There's no one in the water; the red flag flaps wildly over the deserted beach. Driven by an infantile desire for extreme challenges and an inclination toward displays of bravado, feeling like a true swimmer compared to my delicate friend Carlo, and pursued by Franca's familiar cutting remarks, I head out with him toward the mouth of the bay, where the waves break in a deafening crash. Suddenly we're being pulled out to sea. I can discern the rolling hills of the coastline; they emerge and then disappear under an avalanche of water that pulls me down in turbulent cascades. I keep afloat by using my arms and desperately treading water. Let yourself be carried to shore by the current, I remember thinking; it's crazy to swim against it. I recall the losing struggle of trying to fight the undertow, my mouth filling with water, thinking that I'll try again farther down the coast. The shore flashes into sight in a whitish stormy light; the coastline is getting farther away.

Suddenly I hear a feeble cry: Carlo is being consumed by a frothy vortex; he's panicking; he's losing his head; he's calling me in a strange voice. I manage to swim toward him before a wave crashes over me, I come to the surface and grab his arm. His face is green, his mouth twisted in a senseless smile. I grab him under his arms. "Easy now, Carlo, easy," I say. He offers no resistance, and thankfully he doesn't pull me down. I swallow water; the sea opens in an abyss beneath us, it crashes over us; I swallow water again while trying to stay close to the light, close to the froth. Carlo is immobile, paralyzed with fear but close by. I dive down and push him to the surface. When I come up, between sprays of water, I see the coastline again, now even farther away. It's over, I think. How idiotic. We can't both be saved and I can't abandon him; we'll both end up dying. Five minutes ago I was on the beach. The wave picks us up again. I try to hold on to him by his arm, but he slips away and disappears beneath the surface again. I feel his body between my legs so I wrap them around him, dive down and push him up, and come to the surface. I'm shaking. We're being pulled still farther out by the undertow, and the waves are getting even stronger. I reach for his torso but lose my breath. I'm rasping. I hug him; his eyes are glassy. The swollen waves glide beneath us, the shore only an intermittent strip of land. So this is how you die.

Then I see a dark spot on the water; the surface rises up and forms a point. The crest of a wave breaks beyond us. The tip grows larger; it's a rowboat. A man is shouting at us, he leans forward over the oars, the boat tips dangerously, it's about to capsize, it slides back down on a surge, now it's coming closer. I recognize the lifeguard—Come on, Carlo, you can do it—but he doesn't move; maybe it's better that way. I gather my strength as the rowboat comes closer; it's only a few feet away.

"You dickheads!" the lifeguard shouts. I avoid a breaker as the lifeguard reverses the oars. "Grab him by the legs!" he shouts. I lift Carlo up—he's as stiff as a cadaver—the lifeguard grabs him under his arms and yanks him out of the water; heaving him on board, he slips back but doesn't fall. "Damn!" he shouts, and throws me a life preserver. He's furious. "Now hang on!" he yells, and leans on the oars. The bay is getting closer, the life preserver sinks beneath the waves that crash over my head, I see a mass of bubbles, I breathe, swallow water, and suddenly a shock makes me lose hold of the life preserver. The boat crashes against some rocks, the lifeguard swears, and then manages to free himself, one oar breaks, a wave pushes us, raises us, throws us between the jetties, and we fly through as if on rapids, flung forward. And then, suddenly, we're in the harbor, where the water is calm and the crash of waves distant. I close my eyes.

"You idiot!" I hear Franca yell at me when we get closer to the beach. I can touch the sandy bottom with my feet.

"Carlo!" Veronica comes running into the water, screaming as if he had died. I rest on the life preserver; the others make their way toward us and carry Carlo to the beach. I'm alive, exhausted, blissful, and giddy.

"A complete lunatic," I hear the lifeguard say, pointing at me. As I move from the water to the beach, the insults change into admonishments. Franca, Paolo, and Alfredo wait for me on the boardwalk by the cabins. She looks at me sideways, in profile, still trembling. She's trying to express her rage, participation, commiseration, and exasperation and manages to do so quite well.

Alfredo, because of his age, feels authorized to maintain a haughty silence. Paolo, bobbing along between the festivities and the accusations, slowly asks, "Papa, are you crazy?"

"Who, me?" I reply. "Carlo followed me in!" Franca shakes her head as if face-to-face with extremity.

"What happened to your friend?" the doctor asks me, taking the pipe out of her mouth and tamping at the tobacco with her thumb.

"He was hospitalized for a week," I tell her. "He's all right now, but it wasn't easy."

"What was the problem?"

I give her some of the details: intestinal infection caused by ingestion of water, five days of fever, recurrent nightmares of shipwrecks and drowning. When he woke up, all he could remember were my exhortations to stay calm and the strange effect they had on him. He said he had never felt so relaxed in his life. It had been as if someone were rocking him like a new-born baby. "I know what you mean," I told him; we usually say this when we don't understand what someone is talking about. It had been one of the sweetest experiences of his life, he said. "What about you?" he asked. "I remember that I wanted to protect you," I told him. "I felt resigned." I didn't tell him about the idiotic look on his face. To avoid being pathetic, I also added, "I was ready to knock you out if you had tried to struggle. But there was no need."

"What happened to the lifeguard?" the doctor asked, putting the pipe back in her mouth and curling her upper lip in a movement that pipe smokers share with horses.

"He received a commendation in the newspaper and a medal for saving two lives. But somehow it just doesn't seem right."

"Why not?"

"Because if my friend hadn't been there, I would have been able to save myself," I say, caught between vanity and pride. "And if he had been alone, without me, he would have died."

"Surely you know there are no *ifs* in history," she says, laughing.

The electric lights are switched off in the gym. The light from the street comes in through the window, between the iron bars.

Fernanda comes to the door. The strictest and most trusted of the physiotherapists, she's been at the Center the longest. She's also the most exhausted.

"I'm leaving now," she says.

"What? You're still here?" The doctor pretends to scold her. "Go! Leave!"

Fernanda smiles weakly at this slight hint of camaraderie after a tiring day together.

"Have a nice evening, Frigerio," she says, closing the door.

I say goodbye.

"You have good assistants," I say to the doctor.

"Yes, very good," she replies.

"No men, though."

"We do fine without them," she says, looking at me. "It's better that way." Then, after a slight pause, she adds, "I'm not a lesbian, if that's what you're thinking."

"It never occurred to me," I say.

It's not true. I thought about it almost instantly. It's what men love to think when a woman shows authority, firmness, and professional ambition. But by my second visit to the Center I had heard she had fallen in love with a Chilean physiotherapist who ran off with the contents of her safe. It had been a setup that, magnified by its ridiculousness, had left her both embittered and cruel and served to intensify her incisive ways as well as her generosity.

"I admire you," I tell her.

"And so you should," she says.

The pipe has gone out. She draws on it emptily, sucking in her cheeks in the totemic way common to all smokers.

"Tell me more about Fano. About the effects," she says.

"On who, Franca?"

"No, you." She points at me with the pipe. "You're the one who interests me."

"I had a voracious appetite," I reply. "We had lunch at the restaurant on the beach. After finishing my own plate of pasta, I polished off Franca's too. She was still shaken."

"What sensitivity!"

"Whose, mine or Franca's?"

"Yours," she says, laughing.

"I also felt an enormous surge of energy," I continue. "I was happy about myself. I had been ready to die and I didn't hate the idea. Seems like a good sign, no?"

"Sure, great," she says harshly. "Don't give yourself airs."

"I don't think I do."

"If only you could see yourself," she asserts.

I smile. At moments like these, I like myself enormously. This is getting attractive.

"Anyway, a colleague of yours took care of putting things back into perspective for me," I say.

"Who was that?"

"Dr. Fazio. Do you know her?"

"No." She shakes her head. "Where does she work?"

"At the Olgiati Institute. She's a psychiatrist."

"Since when do you go to a psychiatrist?"

"Ever since I was a child. She's a childhood friend."

Finally she lights the pipe again. Vigorous smoke wraps around her face. She breathes in obstinately.

"What did this psychiatrist friend of yours say?"

"That I have powerful repressive mechanisms."

"That's what she said?" she comments, waving the smoke away with her hand.

"Yes. I'm not sure if I should be flattered," I reply. "She used the adjective *powerful*, but she was talking about repression. I'm not sure where I fit in. What do you think?"

She clenched the pipe in her teeth and said professionally, "How old is your friend?"

"Around my age, thirty-six or thirty-seven."

She thought about that for a moment, the pipe still in her mouth. "I'm ten years older than you."

"Now who's thinking about themselves?"

"Me!" She laughs. "You're right!"

The next evening, at almost the same time, she calls me at home. Franca answers.

"Are you calling to lighten Paolo's schedule? We do think it's a bit much," she says, carefully yet firmly.

She listens for a moment, then says, "No, it's not about us. It's him. He seems a little tired these days."

She shrugs. "So you don't think we should worry about it?" Then she nods and says calmly, "I see."

She raises her gaze toward me. "Oh, you wanted to talk to him. Well, goodbye then. And thank you for everything you're doing for Paolo.

"It's for you," she says, passing me the receiver, annoyed.

"Good evening," I say cordially.

"Your wife is so high-strung," she says, also sounding annoyed. "Tell her not to be so worried. Paolo's making progress. He's giving us all the right signs. We have to keep that in mind."

"That's right."

I signal to Franca to turn off the television.

"Even his reaction was good. I liked it. He called you crazy, if I'm not mistaken."

"That's right."

"It was deserving and well articulated," she went on kindly. "But I'm not calling about the child. It has to do with you."

"What is it?"

"Do you know that this morning I caught myself singing?" There's a tone of complicity in her voice. "It hasn't happened to me for years. And do you know why? Because of Fano."

"Because of Fano?"

Franca looks over with raised eyebrows.

"I thought about what you told me. I thought about what you said you felt for your friend when you thought it was all over."

"That's right," I say, for the third time. I feel slightly embarrassed but I don't want to interrupt, as I usually do, when someone is speaking well of me. But she has already finished.

"That's all," she says. "You should be pleased."

I'm quiet.

"I am," she says.

I don't know what to say. I look for an impossible salvation in a cliché.

"That's nice."

"Oh, please," she exclaims in her usual tone, somewhere between peremptory and friendly. "I'm the one who owes you something. A debt of happiness. Do you know what I mean?"

"Naturally."

Franca knows we're not talking about Paolo. She wanders around the living room as if she's looking for something.

"I thought about what your psychiatrist friend told you, too. What was her name?"

"Fazio."

Franca raises her head.

"Right. You can tell your friend that she doesn't understand a thing about you."

"I'll tell her," I say, laughing.

"That's all for now. I'll see you soon," she says, and hangs up.

I look at the phone in my hand, an absent half-smile on my face. Franca notices.

"You told her about Fano."

"Yes."

Franca walks over to a window and closes it delicately. "What did she say?"

"That thinking about it made her happy."

"Does that surprise you?"

"A little."

Franca crosses over to another window. She leans on the sill and looks out into the darkness. "It's not that strange," she says, without looking at me.

"It's not?" I ask in amazement. Franca's the one who seems strange.

"No," she replies soberly, turning toward me. "I think I understand her."

I wait for her to continue. It's the second time in a matter of minutes.

But she doesn't.

Standardized Tests

He has trouble with math.

"I did too, when I was in school," I say.

"Me too," Franca adds.

That's how we console each other after the first round of testing.

"I never understood math at all," my mother-in-law boldly announces.

I look at her. I'm not sure how to interpret that, whether it's a good sign or a bad one.

"I was terrible at it," she says proudly.

I look down at the ground. It takes so little to transform a conversation into a farce. Just one person. This too is a test.

"All right, Paolo, now listen to me. If I divide one hundred by two, what do I get?"

"Fifty," he replies instantly.

Rapidity doesn't matter. This is the third time we do the

problem. At this point, it's no longer a question of doing the math but remembering words.

"And fifty divided by two?"

"Twenty-five."

"And twenty-five times two?"

"Fifty."

"And fifty times three?"

He stares at me. He's sure, as I am, that he's going to make a mistake.

"Think about it," I say.

When I say that I know he stops thinking. Why do I do it? Is it because he *wants* to make a mistake?

He's nervous. He sticks out his chest and his eyes are shiny. He's falling over a precipice.

"A hundred."

"No!" I slam my fist down on the table. "Why did you say a hundred?"

He looks at me a little less fearfully because he finally made a mistake and because I've finally gotten angry.

"I don't know!" he shouts back, in a strangled voice.

I don't want to give up. It's my one weakness. In life, when there's no alternative, we give up. A lot of people can't wait for anything else. They live so that one day they can give up. There, I'm doing it again. I magnify other people's shortcomings in order to minimize my own.

Why don't I give up? Is it because of me? "No," I say out loud, "it's for him." He looks at me: I'm talking to myself. No, I think to myself, it's for me. He's scared. There has to be a reason. I should be scared too. I am his enemy. And he is mine.

I put my elbow on the table and rest my chin in my hand. After a few seconds I look up.

"Let's try again, Paolo."

He is startled.

"What do you get if you double fifty?"

"A hundred."

"What's half of a hundred?"

"Fifty."

"So far, so good."

I spread out my hands on the table, as if to keep my stability in check as well as my power.

"And half of fifty?"

"Twenty-five."

So far, it's just memory. He's not calculating; he remembers the words. This is not understanding math, it's memorizing what you've heard.

"Why don't you just leave him alone?" Franca interrupts.

She looks pale. She's been listening from the kitchen, but now she comes rushing into the living room, fully exasperated with me and ready to liberate and vindicate him.

Paolo looks at her gratefully; she's his unexpected salvation.

"I'm trying to find out whether he understands math or whether he's just memorizing it." I defend myself with an unnatural smile.

"Why? Do *you* understand math?" she exclaims. "Do *you* understand the concept of numbers? *You*—of all people!"

Her *you* is charged with aggressiveness, desperation, disdain. What could I possibly understand—me, of all people—about math? I always relied on memory. Suddenly I recall the sense of paralysis I experienced when the teacher asked me a *different* question. What constituted an exciting aperture for her always proved to be a fatal one for me. It began with, "So, in other terms. . . ." I hated those other terms. I could never imagine what they were. I could never guess what they were.

"Answer me," Franca urged.

"You're right, it's true." I feel both discomfort and relief.

"Then it's idiotic of you to torment him like this!"

She said idiotic, not idiot. It's less personal; it's a tacit convention between us, a loophole to avoid saying it directly.

"I just wanted to try and get him to reason, not just to remember," I reply. "I think sometimes he makes mistakes on purpose."

"On purpose?"

"He gives up thinking as soon as I get nervous. And then comes the wrong answer, as if to punish himself. Or maybe to punish me."

"I'm so sick of your theories!" she yells. "If that's how it is, why bother insisting?"

"I made a mistake!" I yell back. I pound the arm of my chair with my fist. "Can't I make mistakes too?"

I have never been so proud of my mistakes as at this very moment. So arrogantly proud, and in such a crisis too.

"So cut it out!" she says, grabbing my arm.

I jump to my feet, grab her by the shoulders, and shake her violently. She frees herself from my grasp and yells, "What do you think you're doing?"

"What are *you* doing?"

There's fear and hate in her eyes. I let go of her. She rubs her shoulders as if they were sore and flops down on the chair.

"Don't exaggerate," I say.

I try to control my breathing. I try to reacquire a normal voice. Show calm, especially when you lose it. She's trying to regain hers too. Her breathing is even. She looks blankly into the empty space in front of her.

Paolo has been watching all this. He's scared but fascinated by these irregularly recurring scenes. Franca, sounding as if she had just woken up from a restful nap, calmly asks, "Now, what exactly is the problem?"

The unwritten laws of a relationship force her to speak in a delicate voice and to blank out what has just transpired between us.

"The math tests are the problem," I reply distastefully, both communicative and cordial. "We keep looking for excuses, but the truth is that he just doesn't know how to do these tests."

"Now stay calm," she says, gently placing her hand on my knee. "You always said these kinds of tests were unfair indicators."

"In fact, they are."

"That they're quantitative and that they ignore the emotional mind-set."

"It's stonewalling," I say, following her lead.

"What's stonewalling?"

"What he's doing when he refuses to cooperate."

"He does it with you because you don't know how to deal with him."

"No, he always does it."

"That's not true."

She's silent for a moment. She's bitter, edgy, and poised. Then she turns slowly toward him and says, "Paolo, I want you to try with me."

Paolo looks at her apprehensively. She's changing from his emancipator to assuming my role. She grips the arms of the chair.

I stand up and go to the kitchen. The sky has turned dark; it's still raining. I run the water in the sink and drink a glass of water. I just heard on TV that even bottled water is toxic and that tap water may actually be a little less so.

I go back into the living room and watch her shift her hands from her knees to the table. A cone of light from the overhead lamp falls on them.

"No, Paolo. Now try and stay calm. If sixty times two is a hundred and twenty, what is half of it?"

Paolo looks at me. He's lost. He's looking for help.

"Answer your mother," I say.

He has nowhere else to look. There's no getting out of it.

"Fifty," he answers.

"No!" she shouts. "You remember fifty because your father said it before. Fifty has nothing to do with this."

Paolo lets go of the chair. He turns very red. His lip is trembling.

"Leave him alone," I say. "We'll try later," I add.

She closes her eyes. "All right."

I sit down at the table. She stands up.

"Dinner's in half an hour. OK?"

"Fine."

I take Paolo's hand in mine. His eyes are brimming with tears, but he doesn't cry.

"Now tell me, who's right? Your mother or me?" I ask.

The Singing Principal

When Paolo passes from fifth grade into middle school, I ask that he be placed in a section with some of his classmates. It's an unorthodox request.

The principal greets me with white gloves. That's not a metaphor. No one's sure if she wears them to distinguish herself or because she's afraid of catching something. They're made of white lace. For as long as anyone can remember (which is three years, since she was transferred to this school), she's never taken them off.

She's petite and spirited; she looks positively turgid in her tight dress. She has a bubbly voice. She likes to show off her talent as a singer by performing at the end-of-the-year recital, provoking laughter, confusion, and amusement in the audience. She has a strong character, like most integrated and flamboyant people. She comes toward me in a vaguely theatrical manner, almost like an eighteenth-century dame in an opera by Cimarosa.

"Oh, Professor Frigerio, I've heard so many wonderful things about you and your son Paolo!"

I bow ever so slightly. "Why, thank you."

She motions for me to sit down across from her at her desk. There's a large vase of yellow flowers on each end. I'm not sure what kind they are; I can never remember the names of plants. They might be gladioli. Behind her is an oriental screen: marsh birds flying diagonally across a background of green stylized plants.

"Do you like it?" she asks, turning sideways to look at it.

"Yes, very much."

"I brought it in from home. A distant uncle of mine who spent twenty-one years in the diplomatic corps in China gave it to me." She looks at me for a moment and then adds, "It's not worth very much, but it breaks up the academic environment. You've probably heard how much I detest bureaucracy."

"Yes," I say. "I have."

"So there's no need to worry about your son." She rests her hand on a pile of gray folders. "He'll be in class One-C, with an excellent teacher's aide: Professoressa Molteni. Do you know her?"

"No, but I—"

"She's done excellent work with a child that has—how do you say it?—behavioral problems," she says, interrupting me.

"I see," I say, as I often do when I am entirely unclear about something but still want the conversation to go on. "But that's not the point."

"What is?" she asks in surprise, retreating a bit on her swivel chair.

"I wanted—that is, I would have liked—Paolo to be with some of the children from his fifth grade class. He's grown very attached to them."

"He'll make friends with his new classmates," she says resolutely. "What's the problem?"

"Well, you see, he's the one who asked me about it," I say with some difficulty. "If it wasn't right, I'd be the first one to say no. But it seemed like a reasonable request."

She looks at me carefully. "How many years have you been teaching, Professor Frigerio?"

"Twelve," I say uncomfortably, as if under interrogation.

"I've been teaching for twenty-nine years," she says, calmly but triumphantly. "I hate to admit it because it reveals how old I really am."

She has a malicious air about her. I react too late to what she's said, managing only the hint of a smile.

She lowers her voice. "Experience counts. I know your son will be happy with his new classmates."

"Is there some kind of bureaucratic impediment?" I insist.

"Luck of the draw," she says firmly. It's the immediate response of a superior who wishes to include an inferior in some secret and at the same time maintain her distance. "You're not familiar with statute 328 comma 5 of 1976? Well, I suppose not, seeing that you teach at the high school level."

She who so despises bureaucracy has suddenly become very serious. There's nothing like a statute to delight or humiliate a person.

"What does the statute say?" I ask.

"That first-year middle-school students will be assigned to their classes based on the results of a random drawing. We're all equal in the eyes of the law."

"Yes, but he's not equal to the others," I say.

"Professor Frigerio," she says, losing her patience, "this norm was introduced to do away with discriminatory acts. Now you want to introduce one."

"Yes," I say, "that's right. I'd like to introduce a discriminatory act."

I'm beginning to see a way out of this. Paradoxes have always been of great help when reason fails me.

"Actually, the facts introduce it," I add. "He's *not* equal to the others."

"You are insistent, aren't you?" she says, as if I were insisting on some irregularity. "I never would have imagined you to be the type, Professor Frigerio —"

"Please, Signora Preside, listen to me," I say. The use of her title, both stark and bureaucratic, creates instantaneous equality among diverse ranks. "You can surely guess how I feel about discrimination. But that's exactly why he shouldn't be considered like the others. It would be a kind of discrimination for the others and a new one for him."

"I'm sorry, but I don't follow you," the principal says, shaking her head in a pantomime of confusion.

"Racism is an altogether different thing," I say, branching off into a discussion that I should perhaps avoid but it's already too late. "Recognizing diversity is not a form of racism. It's a duty we all have. Racism, however, draws its diverse laws from the differences between races. But we believe that everyone should have equal rights."

"So far, I follow you," the principal says, with a sigh of relief.

I've always thought that the best way to change someone's mind is to convince them that you're not actually doing it.

"As such, my son is allowed to study within the public school system." There's another linguistic aid that should help convince the principal: the use of the term "public school system." "But he also has the right to be treated with special regard. For example, he doesn't do gym with the other children."

"Naturally!" the principal exclaims.

"And then he's got the teacher's aide to help him," I add.

"That's right," she says emphatically.

"So, if we want to help him just a little bit more, let's permit him to be with some of his old classmates."

She takes her time to reply, knowing all the while that my eyes are fixed on her. Mustering up all the authority she can, she says, "Did you know that your son has been rather unlucky? There's only one of his old classmates in his new class."

"I know."

I say no more. Silence has to work in my favor.

"Well, what can we do about it? You're against the most democratic measure that's been introduced," the principal complains.

"No, it's simply that in this case a random drawing goes against intelligence."

She raises her eyebrows. "And what would you propose to do about it?"

"Violate the law in order to respect the spirit." I'm surprised by my fearlessness. "Change the results of the drawing."

"No," the principal says, sliding even farther back in her chair.

I look at her in dismay, aware that I have asked too much. I chose the wrong words, not the wrong objective. It's always the same thing.

"Let me think about it," she says apprehensively.

There's a large blue globe on a shelf above her desk. It caught my eye when I first walked in: an unappeased dream of my youth.

"Would you mind if I brought the parents' representative in on this?" she asks, pointing toward a door behind her desk. "I asked her to make herself available in case there was a need."

"Fine." I nod.

I'm not sure whom she's seeking to help. Perhaps she's not even sure herself.

She goes out of the room, closing the door behind her. I look at the globe. The midmorning sun shines down on the playground below. There's a warmth in the air, a brightness, the feel of vacation. I imagine the sound of children's voices. It would be time for recess.

"This is our dear friend Professor Frigerio," the principal says, reappearing at the door and gesturing toward me with uneasy kindness. "This is Signora Matteucci."

Signora Matteucci is tall, elegant, and refined. She looks persuasive. She smiles at me knowingly, as if we have already met.

"I explained the situation to Signora Matteucci," the principal says. "She has a degree in psychology. Even she was surprised."

"Don't pay any attention to the degree in psychology," my new enemy says collegially. "I'm not a psychologist. I work part-time in an advertising firm."

"I suppose that's pretty interesting."

"Not as interesting as you'd think," she says; I can tell she really works there. "But let's talk about your case." She crosses her legs and folds her hands gently over her knees. Her smile is not promising. "So. You'd like special privileges for your son, is that right?"

It couldn't have begun any worse. I smile and shake my head.

"Well, then, why don't you explain things to me."

"I'll start with a given," I say. "The state wants to integrate disabled children into the system instead of isolating them in special schools."

"Yes, that's right," she concedes placidly.

I'm using the jargon that I abhor, that of my interlocutors. I know it strips me of my strengths and credibility even as I acquire it in their eyes. I alter my course.

"Look, Paolo is disabled. He'll have a teacher's aide," I say heatedly. "I'd like him to have the aid of his friends too."

"Why, Professor Frigerio? Tell me why," Signor Matteucci says with profound calmness and curiosity. She leans toward me as if I were telling her a secret. "Why does your son need his old classmates so much?"

"They need him too!" I say. "Naturally, his classmates have provided him with friendship, solidarity, and admiration. But he's given them a lot as well. Having him in the class has been an added encouragement for them, a kind of stimulus. That's what his teacher always said. It might have been out of compensation, perhaps, but what difference does that make?"

"I believe you." Signora Matteucci nods, opening her eyes wide. Many women do that; they think it has a special effect.

"It was entirely unexpected," I go on to say. "A class that benefited from a disabled student as much as he benefited from them. Why do we have to interrupt this experience?"

"But who's interrupting it, Professor Frigerio?" Signora Matteucci asks, in an amazed yet pedantic tone. "Your son will enjoy other equally positive interpersonal relationships."

"Yes, but he suffers from a particular kind of anxiety." I'm unsure which point to give more importance. "The thought of losing his friends, who in turn will find themselves together in another class, seems unfair to him—"

"It's up to you to convince him otherwise," the principal interrupts.

"I agree," I say, "but why complicate his life more than necessary because of a random drawing?"

"Now calm down, Professor Frigerio," the principal replies

loudly. "I can understand your frame of mind, but we do not invent the rules."

"I understand," I say. "No one knows that as well as I do." How did I come up with that one? "But it's ridiculous to chain ourselves to a lottery."

"Why?" the principal asks with genuine surprise. "How often has it happened in history?"

Now I'm the one who looks at her in amazement. I can tell this is not the path to take.

"Let's think about this calmly, Frigerio," Signora Matteucci suggests gently. She has dropped the title of professor, which gives her leave to speak to me in a more confidential, even intimate, manner. "Talk to me—but be sincere. Please!"

"All right," I said, nodding.

I know from experience that invitations to sincerity invariably hide aggressive impulses.

"Why do you fear new classmates for your son, Frigerio?"

"He's the one who fears them. Actually, no, he doesn't fear them; he'd just like to be with a few old classmates. They were connected. They protected him."

"Now there's the key word," Signora Matteucci exclaims with careful enthusiasm, looking up at me. "Protection! You want to protect your son too much. But he has to face life." Then, as if relinquishing herself to an irresistible novelty, she adds, "Life is all about risks!"

I listen to her in astonishment. There will always be someone to point out the road that you take every day. They'll tell you that they do it in your best interest, and ultimately you end up having to thank them.

Signora Matteucci can't resist sinking the knife in a little bit deeper. "It's not that you want to protect yourself, Frigerio, is it? And that the child is a projection of your own fears?"

"Who, me?" I look down. "No, believe me. The problem is very simple. It's a problem of common sense."

I use this word in desperation. It had always seemed like abnegation to me, but here it's turning into a conquest. But never jump to conclusions. We credit people with intelligence they don't really have. It happens all the time.

The two women are looking at each other, and that seems like a positive sign. But then Signora Matteucci demurs.

"Frigerio, you're not taking advantage of your role as a teacher, are you, to ask us for this infraction of the norm?"

"Taking advantage?" I look up. "I don't really think that's the right word."

"You're right, I meant something else, but you know what I mean."

I nod, even if I don't really understand. Maybe she chose the wrong term on purpose so she could correct herself.

"Still, it is a problem," the principal says in alarm. "How do we get out of the drawing? It's the law, after all."

"You don't have to get out of it," I say confidently. "It's just that the drawing will have a more intelligent outcome. Why should we accept a stupid drawing?"

"Because it's a drawing," she says.

"And we, who are more important than a drawing, can modify it. It's enough to read a D instead of a C. A pen mark is enough."

"How very removed you are from it all, Frigerio!" the principal exclaims.

She's given up on the title now, too, and this makes me feel better.

"What do you think?" she asks, turning toward Signora Matteucci.

"Nothing. I don't know a thing about it. Never saw a thing."

I lean back in my chair.

"Section D, you said?" the principal asks, to be sure.

"Yes. Thank you."

"For what?" she asks.

Matteucci (I leave off the Signora too, when I say goodbye) disappears again through the little door behind the desk. I have participated in a drama; I'm a wreck, I'm happy, I'm depressed. I've won a small victory in a war that is destined never to be over.

I take leave of the principal. On the way out, I can't resist reaching up and touching the globe. I spin it slowly in a counterclockwise direction.

Death of an Actress

My mother died when Paolo was still learning to walk. I don't think she'd like that as a start to her obituary. Even though she continued to dedicate her energies toward this goal up to the very end (she helped Franca every day with Paolo's exercises in an indefatigable competition with my mother-in-law), she always had an exclusive sense of her own personal destiny. Although the love she felt for her grandson was relentless, it still didn't complete—to use a favorite metaphor of hers—the scene. We tend to think that our parents exist as a function of ourselves, and when they don't, we repay them with inextinguishable hate—at least until we reach their age, when their perspective becomes ours. But by then it's usually too late to tell them.

My mother, who spoke as if I had learned how to walk at the age of nine months, waited nine years in vain. Ambitious and bitter, never content with the cards that life had dealt her, wounded by what she had been denied, she put hyperbolic meaning into the humiliations to which she was subjected. Paolo, unsteadily taking his first steps, was to be seen as a champion, with utter admiration. She made her friends share in these triumphs. The tears that occasionally fell from her eyes were the only sign of her torment; they were enough to offset the disquiet that she felt upon his successes. If it's solidarity you're after, it's good to let some kind of passive voice inhabit your stories. People will always be grateful for it. And you know they never love you as much as when you're not doing well.

A dilettante in an amateur theater group in the town where she grew up, my mother never entirely abdicated her destiny as an actress. She simply sacrificed it in the name of pride. Julius Caesar, who would rather have been the top dog in a small town than an underdog in Rome, succeeded in becoming the top dog in Rome. But because my mother was afraid of not being able to emulate him in the capital, she gave up on the town. That was the difference between Caesar and my mother: he would have been happy with the town.

After giving up on the idea of making the theater her life, she decided to transform her life into theater. She loved ceremonies, parties, and receptions of all kinds. My father, a commanding officer in the Carabinieri, was originally seduced by her theatrical career but slowly came to find it nauseating. Believing that he shared in it, he never opposed what he saw as her aesthetic existence, although he never really understood, even at the very end, just how foreign aesthetics were to their lives. While my mother, during one of their parties, would stroll radiantly through an apartment far too small for her ambitions, he would withdraw into a corner, his unwavering stare revealing his struggle to stay awake. I never asked whether he betrayed her, a question children never raise until they, themselves, consider betrayal. And when they finally do ask, they discover virtual abysses in their parents' pasts, hypothetical dramas and comedies performed with simulated patience. When I asked myself about it, I could never come up with an answer. He was much older than she, a fact that revealed just as much as if he had been younger. I continue to delude myself, however, that I can retrospectively interpret my mother's behavior.

Despite the dramatic tone of the epitaph my mother had inscribed on his tombstone—*struck down by untimely death*—my father left her longing less for his person than for the uniform that he had worn. That's what she remained faithful to, dreaming in her patriotically visionary way that she had been the lifetime companion of a hero.

When he was accidentally killed during a military exercise, she shut herself off in theatrical mourning for years, raising her children to venerate his memory. As happens with many widows, her conjugal life became more desirable in retrospect than it actually had been, mainly because it was over.

I don't think I could ever rise to such deification in the eyes of my two sons. Franca would never contribute to it, the boys would be stunned, and I along with them. As for my mother, my repudiation of any kind of uniform was the exact opposite of what she had hoped for.

That's how domestic gods are born. And that's how they fade.

Periodically, when the fatigue of Paolo's rehabilitative therapy and life with us would make itself felt, my mother would return to her own house. She lived in the *hinterland*, a word she had easily adopted, perhaps because she thought it ennobled her degraded Italian suburb with a touch of English. She shared the house with a woman her age, the widow of a pensioned police captain. They had nothing in common except a garden. And yet, over time, they learned to get along, each conceding superiority to the other in a subject they cared little for: my mother took culture, the other woman got common sense. Each of them secretly doubted the legitimacy of this division and would let it show in sarcastic comments. Still, they learned how to distance their skepticism for the benefit of a common good that the passing years made more important than anything else: armistice.

My father-in-law often drove Paolo out to her house. Sometimes I'd go with them. She would stand under the arbor and welcome us. She always commented on what enormous progress her grandson was making, but her enthusiasm ultimately frustrated me. If she had simply said *progress*, I would have believed her. Excess reveals lies; truth doesn't want superlatives.

Her hospitality followed the pattern of ancient rituals. False surprise, followed by apologies for the disorderly state of things, the offering of a frugal yet accurately calculated lunch (always the same). In her *asides*, not onstage with her guests but in the solitary zones of her garden, she revealed her deeper humanity. Everything that makes up man is human, but *humanity* has a stronger, more mysterious sense. It forces us to surrender in the face of truth. Standing in a corner of the garden, between the sharp angle of the renovated chicken coop and the plastic garden chairs stacked by the robinia hedge, my mother surrendered to truth. She told me, for example, that she was no longer sure she would see my father again. For a fatally fanatic believer such as herself—or, rather, for someone who was completely intolerant of her own doubts—it was an unexpected admission. Nor did she seem too upset about it; that was another sign of her belated sincerity. "I'm not sure of anything anymore," she confided to me one day, pouring hot chocolate into one of the cups that were part of the service she bought in Faenza in 1932.

On another occasion, a quiet and breezy September afternoon with the wind blowing through the fruit trees, she confessed wearily, "Do you know why I don't want to die? Because of the sun."

I wasn't sure if this was a domestic revival of the sun as adored by the Egyptians or a rephrasing of the words she had uttered as Antigone sixty years earlier or one of her anthropocentric-cosmic intuitions. Perhaps it was simply an expression of solitude warmed by her domestic environment, by the long afternoons that she spent in the garden, sitting by the fence and watching the cars drive up the ramp onto the highway.

In her final months, my mother began to see time as if through a lens. She no longer lived from day to day but from hour to hour. She had reached ninety, an age she had imperiously assigned to destiny, and considered herself a survivor. She adhered to the present with a disconcerting intensity, with neither regrets nor hopes.

She tended a small vegetable patch in a distant corner of the garden. She looked dreamy, like she did when I was a child. Although I had never shared in her illusions, I began to listen carefully to her anecdotes about the growth of vegetables. She had become a minor visionary.

She became more understanding about Paolo's handicap. At first she had hated it, but now she loved his serenity. She no longer asked what he couldn't do but rather what he enjoyed, what made him feel good. And the tears that ran down her smiling face were of melancholy joy.

I like to think she would have enjoyed hearing what the old priest said on the morning of her funeral. He spoke about life, not death; about the resurrection of the body, not of its dissolution; about the brilliant light, not the darkness. He spoke with a happiness that threatened to disturb the masks of those present, both the more serene ones of family members and the serious, austere ones worn by the tourists of mourning. He didn't say anything about *her*. That seemed like a providential sign. It would only have been inadequate.

On leaving the church after that unusual ceremony, more of an ancient ritual than a metropolitan one, more of a festivity than a funeral, it was as if we were accompanying her on a last stroll through the countryside. As we walked behind the hearse on that clear June morning down narrow country roads, flanked on either side by old stone walls, shaded by the trees, I found myself thinking about the sun and how she had learned to love it, how it shone through the branches, so distant and yet so near.

A Late Consultation

Among the many doctors who attended to Paolo, I recall one in particular about whom I have forgotten practically everything — his name, his face, the circumstances of the appointment. We went to him, I think, when Paolo was about thirteen. He was a famous specialist with a wealth of experience; a mutual friend had suggested him. We were hoping to get some kind of support and encouragement for the regimen we had been following, and possibly some clear suggestions that would accelerate the undeniable progress Paolo had made so far. I can barely remember where his office was located, nor do I recall any particular details about it, although often I'm more interested in the surroundings than in the occupants themselves. I do recall that we were feeling somewhat less tormented by the distressing thought of the future, a thought that never leaves those with a disabled child, and waited calmly for our consultation.

All I remember is his opinion, which I will here transcribe in the manner of the ancient historiographers (even though they don't always make this explicit), which is to say, I'll use my words to reproduce the unequivocal sense of his:

"I'm sorry, truly sorry, for all the work that you—and above all you, Signora—have done up until this point, but it has been entirely useless. I have absolutely no faith in the Doman method. Its only worthwhile characteristic is to accelerate the progress that the child would inevitably make on his own. To rotate the child's head one hundred and eighty degrees several hundred times a day and to bombard his brain with stimuli will certainly have some effect. But so would a continual caress on his toe or a walk through the park in his wheelchair. The powerfully reactive physiology of the child knows far more than the aggressive Doman therapy. I know this may come as a bitter surprise to you, but the child, as far as I can tell, has made progress. Is it so very important to know why?"

It's very possible that he then turned toward us and smiled, feeling both accountable for and proudly deferential to his own knowledge.

It just so happens that I remember our reaction—perhaps it was not as casual as I would think—and it surprised both of us. Man is always unpredictable. It was as if we had been dealt a trick that had been intended for someone else. The speech didn't upset us, as its author had hoped it would (today, years later, I can see that). I would never say to one of my ex-students that all their work had been futile and they would have learned more if they had opted for another path than the one they had so laboriously undertaken. Often cruelty is dubbed unconscious only because it hides behind a smile; the blade sinks in between the ribs, but the person who knifed you is holding you up so lovingly and thoughtfully! As for doctors—with the exclusion of the very best—they have the additional alibi of sincerity (another is stupidity, but they don't know that). The specialist we met with on that occasion had gotten a thrill out of telling us that our ten years of work had been a waste, yet it was precisely that perception that debased him and tipped the balance of credibility. Doubtless he had exaggerated because he found it paradoxically pleasing to be cordially hostile. And somehow this delicate ferocity was reassuring.

I am reminded of a story by Maupassant, I think it's called "The Necklace." In the story, the protagonist, after sacrificing years of his life to pay off a debt for a diamond necklace that someone had lent him and which he promptly lost, discovers, at the end, that the necklace was a fake. We didn't react with panic, we didn't even have retrospective panic, and this defined the difference between the two situations. Those years had been like climbing a mountain—for Paolo as well as for us—and they had given us hope. Through the daily torture of obsessive gymnastics we had probably transmitted to him our irresponsible faith in his recovery. This, in light of the results we obtained, must have counted for something.

We never talked about that doctor again. Nor does the threat of the return of repressed memories haunt us. Maybe we didn't repress his memory. Maybe we just forgot about him. Still the doctor was right about some things.

It was just him. He himself was wrong.

All in Good Time

"Yes, like all boys his age," Franca says.

"How do you know?"

We're sitting in Paolo's room. He's down in the courtyard, learning to ride the moped. She points to his bed.

"I make it every day."

"And you're sure it's not a case of nocturnal bedwetting."

"No, it is not nocturnal bedwetting."

"Have you seen him do it?"

She looks at me impatiently. "No, but it's as if I have."

I try to seem indifferent but I'm not. "It's normal," I say with a nod. I don't know whether to feel relieved or upset.

"You should talk to him about it," she says.

"About what?"

"Not about that," she says seriously. "About the subject generally. It might help him mature a little."

"Why, does he seem infantile to you?"

"Please, don't start," she exclaims. "The doctor told you he's intelligent. The only thing you worry about is his intelligence!"

I try not to look at her. "I worry about the important things."

"Fine, but you have to remember that his knowledge is limited compared to other children his age. That's why you should talk to him."

"Do you think it would do him good?"

"Yes," she says, surprising herself. "He listens to you," she says, with conjugal disbelief.

I am silent.

"Besides, you are a teacher, aren't you? Teach your son something!"

"All right," I say, also in disbelief.

He's lying on the bed, with a pillow behind his head, knees bent, feet together.

"Paolo, don't you think we should have a little talk?"

That's the essential proposition behind the most important problems, the kinds we have the least amount of time for.

He frowns apprehensively, clearly unwilling.

He makes me feel like a badly timed visitor, one of those people who calls at dinnertime, just as you're sitting down to eat, because, they confess, they know they'll find you at home. My thoughts go to a friend of mine who told me about the inexplicable resistance that she encountered in her daughter. "It doesn't come as a surprise, knowing you," I had said. Then after a moment of seriousness, I had said, "Don't you think that dialogue has to include silence?"

I am making the same mistake.

"OK," he says, sitting up with difficulty on the bed. "What do you want to talk about?"

"About your relationship with girls."

I've acquired a detached tone, as if I am pursuing a strange idea that has suddenly crossed my mind.

His legs flinch but then are still.

"Do you want to talk about it?"

He nods.

"You know why I'm asking you?" I say. "Because when I was your age, I didn't know anything about it either."

It's true. He looks at me with some concern. I had figured out some of the pieces of the puzzle, but I didn't know how they fit together. I remember thinking that women had some kind of pump into which they sucked men. Absurd—yet almost true.

"You're a good-looking boy. You have problems walking and speaking, but still, girls will like you."

He nods tentatively.

"You have a great sense of humor and you're very kind. Girls like that. You're gallant, too."

I wink at him, and he smiles for the first time.

"What else do you need to win them over?"

I take for granted that he's missing something. He retreats into a state of unease. Another mistake is asking him for the answer you should be providing.

"Maybe there is something that you're missing."

He looks at me with detached curiosity. He knows adults ask questions so that they can answer them themselves.

"A tiny bit of malice," I add. "You have to make them curious. You have to try and surprise them."

I'm telling him exactly what my mother, who used to get involved in my relationships, would tell me about women when I was his age. She talked about them as if they had programmable reactions. She even showed a certain disdain for them, but no less than that which she reserved for men.

Paolo is perplexed.

"You have to be less childish," I say. "Sometimes you're a little repetitive."

"You are too, sometimes."

He knows that turning against me always works. I laugh. He's gaining territory. Maybe that's what I want.

"But, you see, that's not the point," I go on to say. "All men are, in some ways, infantile. We never really leave infancy. We stayed there for too long."

He listens carefully. We talk less about him and more about men in general. I feel more interested in what I am saying. Do we teach only when we're interested?

"That's why women don't mind when men are infantile. Just not too much and not always."

He doesn't say anything, but I think he agrees with me.

"You should try and meet one of those altruistic girls who are willing to face certain difficulties. Not that there aren't nasty surprises with them too."

"There aren't?"

He quiets down when situations become complicated and when his case fits into the category of universal complications.

"Anyway, you know what I mean," I say, to get out of my embarrassed muddle.

"No."

We both laugh. Maybe we didn't understand each other, but we've come to an understanding.

He takes advantage of the situation to make the last remark, which at this moment is very important to him—and helps me out—by saying, "All in good time, Papa."

You Didn't Think
I Could Do It, Did You?

Paolo used to say it on various occasions between the ages of ten and fifteen, like the time I had gone ahead to press the call button and he made it up the three stairs that lead to the elevator from the lobby without my help. "You didn't think I could do it, did you?" Or when he poured himself a glass of water without spilling a drop, his trembling hand still on the bottle. Or when he managed to throw a rubber ball into a wide basket without falling and hitting the back of his head on the gym mat. Or when he managed to buy tickets for a concert over the phone without having the operator hang up on him. Sometimes they'd interpret his slow and, at times, inarticulate voice for a prank call and hang up. Sometimes they'd ask him to repeat what he had said, ultimately with the same outcome. He'd break out in a sweat, his eyes would burn with determination, but he wouldn't give up. It made me simultaneously proud and exasperated. I remember wanting to get on the phone and scream at the operator to listen more carefully and not resort to "I'm sorry, I don't understand"—which so many people say complacently rather than regretfully.

"No, I really didn't think you could," I'd reply, with excessive enthusiasm for my own sincerity. Then one day I realized that my reaction made him unhappy. It was as if I were constantly opening up a wound that he wanted to heal. He'd blush with a kind of retrospective melancholy that would poison the pleasure of the moment. His eyes would flash with an uneasy presentiment, as if an inextinguishable fear was being confirmed. I was trying to valorize the present, but this made the past even less bearable. To have one's capabilities questioned by those for whom one cares the most is an atrocious experience. We've all been through it. It may have fortified us against our own backsliding, but we paid for it in grim coinage, denying ourselves and others the pleasure of unself-consciousness.

Paolo didn't want me to reinforce the sense of mistrust that so many parents have about their children's development. In his repetitive and ingenious way, he hoped the present would free him from the past and the unappealable sentence that had been pronounced on his future could be modified with retroactive measures. Then, one evening, I thought about what a literature professor of mine had once told me in a vehement attack of stupidity and cruelty: "You'll never know how to write!" It was a verdict I never forgot, and its unfairness has persecuted me ever since. That's when I understood that I had to modify the past for Paolo in order to make it acceptable to him (it was no longer possible to do so with my own). So I told him, with that truthfulness that we find only when we're altering the truth, "You see, it's not that I didn't believe in you. I hoped you would be able to do it, but I didn't want to deceive myself. I knew that if I deceived myself I would get impatient with your mistakes. That's why, even at the risk of going against my instincts, I preferred to be downbeat. Do you understand?"

I'm not sure he understood. Often, all people can intuit is that we are disturbed and we want to help. So they give us back that which we need most: their help.

From then on, Paolo never asked that question again.

A Girl on the Phone

He's on the telephone. He turns pale and starts stuttering. He's perspiring; his eyes are shiny.

"It's a girl," Franca whispers, passing me in the hallway.

He looks down and in his hoarse, slow voice he asks, "What's your name?"

He listens silently. His breathing is slow and heavy. Then, perplexed, he says, "No, I don't remember."

He looks up and sees me. He looks away.

He takes a breath. Usually, if I'm around, I'll gesture to him to reply quickly so that his interlocutor doesn't get bored. But now I don't say a word.

"So where do you want to meet?" he asks her slowly, but with a slightly knowing tone.

She must not have understood him because he repeats the sentence even slower.

He waits in trepidation. I'd like to run over and hug him.

"When?" he asks.

Then he looks at the receiver in his hand, stupefied and dismayed. I sit down next to him.

145

"Did she hang up?"

"Yes," he says.

"Do you know her?"

He shakes his head. I'm afraid he's going to cry.

I don't know what to say, except the truth. Immediately. At least the truth.

"It's a joke, Paolo. Don't take it seriously."

He nods.

"It's a stupid joke. They used to do it when I was in school, too. Girls would call up boys from another class so they wouldn't know who they were."

I'm lying. (Speaking of truth!) But it could have been true.

"React!" I insist. "Don't pay any attention to her. She's stupid. Next time just tell her so."

"No," he says, looking at me.

"Yes, you have to! You need to know that there are stupid girls out there. Don't make room for them."

"But love is important," he says, his voice at first choked up and then clear. "Maybe you didn't know that," he adds.

He tries to wriggle away from me, but I've grabbed him by the shoulders.

"No, Paolo, I do know it."

"She spoke to me about—"

I know I have to distract him. I can't give in. If he were to see me get emotional it would only make things worse.

"She's a kid; you have to pity her," I say, taking his hand in mine. "It was a stupid joke, but I don't hate her either."

He looks at me in amazement.

"That's right, it was stupid of her to play a joke on you," I say. "It was cruel. But she's treating you the same way she would treat the others. Don't feel sorry for yourself, all right? We don't have to like her, but worse things can happen."

I don't know what I'm saying but I've succeeded in distracting him. And something I said must have comforted him. He's calmer now.

"When she grows up, she'll be the first one to understand how stupid she was," I add.

The punch line doesn't convince him. I fatally pronounced the additional word that manages to diminish all the others. Why bet on the girl's future? Why so much deferred kindness?

"No, you're right, Paolo," I say. "She may end up being stupid for the rest of her life. There are so many stupid people in the world. Do you think any of them were smart as children?"

He starts to smile.

"There, that's the way," I say. "It's not worth wondering why she did it."

Suddenly, the expression on his face becomes serious. He's disappointed.

"She did it because I'm disabled," he says, in a low voice.

Prayer

Until Paolo was two years old, we believed that his recovery had to be complete. That's what I asked for in my prayers on Sundays. I started going to mass again after many years. An inner voice (I heard it clearly, almost physically, and it didn't sound like my own) had convinced me that my prayers would be heard.

Later on, I mitigated my request. I did away with the adjective *complete*. I was ready to settle for *partial*. I was ready, in my passionate and erratic dealings with the all-powerful, to accept a disability in Paolo. Concessions (I'm not sure whose, my own or the Almighty's) that once would have seemed atrocious—his condition was much worse, we learned, than what we originally had expected—had become acceptable. After a very long silence, I heard the voice say, *Yes, it will come to pass.*

I left that encounter feeling heartened. I also felt pleased with my cunning. I didn't make any promises that I knew I wouldn't be able to keep. No, I wouldn't leave her. I didn't promise that. I

couldn't lose her purely as a result of my own unilateral deci-
sion, nor was I ready for an amputation I wouldn't know how to
live with. But, for that matter, the Almighty wasn't asking me to
leave her either. I felt pretty confident that he would tolerate it,
though I certainly didn't want to subject him—and myself—to
the test. What on earth would I have done if he had said no?

I realize that this way of praying might seem absurd and irresponsible. In its defense I can only say it was my own. I won't say
anything about the rapture and fervor and devotion with which
I prayed. I'll leave that—as a narrator might once have said so
as not to fall into a trap—to the reader's imagination. Other
people, these days especially, would talk about it, but I'm not
sure the reader actually benefits. Emotions are besieged by com-
motion, which veils the sight and makes the voice falter. It's
enough for the reader to dip into his or her own experience to
understand. One thing is sure; I didn't pray to the Almighty with
my hands stuffed in my pockets.

I made concessions, however, in the frequency with which
I met her. I would see her one time less per week, even if this
meant having to deal with her, and she didn't care at all about
my dealings with the Almighty. I also made certain sacrifices
in my eating habits, which, all told, weren't bad for my diet. I
never would have been able to impose them otherwise. Here,
for this utilitarian compromise, I think I counted on the long-
suffering indulgence of my Interlocutor. Not on his distraction,
given his omniscience.

I'm not sure where I picked up this paranoid method of measur-
ing giving and having. Maybe as a child, in the religious schools
I went to, where we were taught that a final and divine justice
guarantees the remuneration of all our covenants. When you

compare this method to that of the Romans—the way their military commanders would hide in their tents before battle in order to avoid seeing any inauspicious signs from the gods that would have forced them to alter their plan of attack—I suppose it can be considered progress. I had been tempered by the centuries, perhaps. I chose not to follow formal legalism but opted for a softer approach.

I did ask for a miraculous recovery, recalling how, in Scriptures, it had been obtained through faith. But what exactly was my faith like? Intermittent and undulant: intense in times of need and circumspect and tenuous in others. When we ask ourselves if the *ancients* truly believed, we should be asking ourselves how *we* believe.

There was something overwhelming in my need to pray, a need as inevitable as it was contentious. It didn't disturb me that my reason considered this need irreducible; it only served to make the need more evident. This was the perception of things that I had when I prayed; it was like the blinding glare of a lighthouse only a few meters away. Gradually, as I distanced myself, the light would diminish into the night or dissolve into the light of day. I would hear the words of Scripture that dismiss the faithful—"Go now, and you shall be healed"—but I felt them to be true only when I was close to the light. By the time I returned to the apartment, which had been transformed into a neurotic gym because of the slow rate of progress, the light was no longer with me. Only now, some thirty years later, can I begin to understand or acquire more patience, at least retrospectively. When we're young we ask God for everything and immediately, because God is young too. When we grow older, it takes God a bit longer to get things done. After all, that's why we've got time—to help us mature. Recently I went to see a young homeopath for something that had been bothering me. "Will it heal?" I found myself asking him. "Heal?" he said in amazement. "Think about death and you'll see that the verb *heal* doesn't have the weight you attribute to it."

I nodded, amazed at how this person thirty years younger than myself had reflected so proficiently on the theme of healing. Even so, I changed doctors.

His words did help me understand that we never recover completely from stupidity. I changed my mind about praying, as I did about healing. Perhaps prayer and healing converge. Prayer is healing—not from pain but from desperation. Only prayer can interrupt the solitude of dying.

Still now, prayer puts me in touch with a voice that answers. I don't know what it is. But it's a deeper and more lasting voice than the one that tries to deny it. And each time I have denied it, I've rediscovered it in more difficult times. And it wasn't an echo.

I know that both survivors and the dying pray. I know that winners pray as well as those who enter a losing battle. I gave up celestial accounting a long time ago; I gave up the balance sheets of giving and having; I gave up the fiscal expectations of the divine.

I'll be content (a fitting adjective—both melancholy and lucid) with a final encounter with the voice. When all else is lost, I know it'll still be there.

A disabled person has faith by way of compensation. That's what other people think, anyway. Nor does this interpretation, which is both astute and generous, lack coherence. If we all turn to the Almighty in times of need (as happens in human relationships), who needs him more than a disabled person whose life requires constant assistance? This would confirm that my relationship with the Almighty is not so unusual.

"How very fortunate," they say about Paolo's faith. "Otherwise, in his condition . . ." the more sensitive among them delicately add, without completing the sentence. "What a wonderful help," the most euphoric say. The cynics, feeling even more lucid than the others, take up Voltaire: "If it didn't exist, it would have to be invented." They don't think about themselves, they think about him. It's the marginal utility of the disabled, an economist of social pain would say. They are part of the collective delegate that suffers for others, and their burden is so large because it embraces the universal. The reality of it is only slightly different. Disabled people, accustomed to living with deformation—and to putting up with it—don't have the same untenable image of it that those who are healthy do. Faith, for them, is not an escape but a conquest.

The poor will inherit the kingdom of heaven; that's not such a bad trade-off. He who inherits the earth, even a little portion of it, has nothing to complain about but always does. That's the grotesque side to a relationship in which the person doing the commiserating is actually the first one who deserves commiseration. Beware of telling him so, though. The person who shows pity toward others never imagines that he or she actually inspires it. That's how they exorcise it from their lives. That's how they try to distance it, when actually it's the fastest way to earn it.

I know Paolo is attracted to ceremonies of all kinds. He prefers the festive ones, such as baptisms, communions, and weddings, but even funerals fill him with gratifying compunction. I pointed it out to him once, lightly and ironically, but he didn't appreciate it.

He's also good—people say—at *consoling* friends and relatives, a classic ritual that has fallen into disuse. He uses the resources of his slow and irregular voice to pronounce words that seem to come from some remote place, creating an emotional reaction in those who hear him. I am both proud and disturbed by this. I wouldn't want these people to overestimate the strength of his words just because the vessel that transmits them is weak.

I decide to be sincere with him (in other words *I need him*) and I confess that this news makes me both glad and concerned. He looks at me with resignation and disappointment. Then, his voice weary, he says, "It surprises you, doesn't it?"

Once, in smiling solemnity, he said something that had a scriptural quality to it: "You are not the only teacher."

I find myself turning to him as an intermediary. You can tell I subscribe to the belief, without really knowing why, that people with problems have insider access to the Almighty. And that the Almighty is, in turn, easily influenced. I am so struck by this thought that I try to defend myself by imagining just how many people believe it. As a result, I magnify it to such a degree that a collective absurdity casts its shadow (or its light?) over me.

He looks at me and intuits the tortuous paths I have traveled in order to arrive at this request. He replies with a sentence he might have heard at mass or at a meeting of the church youth group (in trying to judge our children objectively we oscillate between beneficent megalomania and apprehensive underestimation). He has the power, however, of making the words his own at just the right time, which is how he manifests his originality.

"Prayer isn't magic, you know."

Able and Disable

To use a rash euphemism, Paolo doesn't have good memories of one of the doctors at the Center. He continues to remember him with hate not only because he loathed his irony but because he was incapable of responding to it. An offense becomes intolerable when we add to it the embarrassment of weakness.

From what he told me I could tell that when it happened he'd feel paralyzed, like an insect caught in a spider's web. It happened to me too when I was young, during my stint in the military, with a sublieutenant who was as uncouth as he was shrewd, as pusillanimous as he was mocking. Never would I have been able to convince him of my worth. With those who want to deny us, there's always going to be a desperate struggle. The more we seek to prove ourselves, the more the other, intuiting our need to do so, denies us. And he's the one we always want to convince; he is the incarnation of our invincible enemy, the one we suppress inside.

Paolo didn't know how to respond to the doctor's sarcastic remarks when he was accused, for example, of preferring his church youth group to the Center.

"But it's true," I tell him placidly, trying to induce him to think objectively. When we're right, we like frustrating others — children and parents alike.

"No!" he burst out saying. "He was just teasing!"

I look at him incredulously. He's exaggerating. He knows I enjoy his taste for hyperbole.

"He was being terrible! You have to make him pay for it!"

"Are you joking?" I ask.

I don't know if I should entertain the maturity of a game or the immaturity of a deferred vendetta.

He looks at me to see whether I'm joking too.

"Yes and no," he says.

He's always divinely ambivalent, both infantile and knowing, subtle and simple. He understands that a coexistence of contraries provides its own access to knowledge.

"So he was just teasing a bit. What harm is there in that?"

"No, he was being perfidious."

His expression is serious until he sees me smile.

"He had a small brain," he adds excitedly. Every shot that hits the mark is for him a conquest.

"Now you're exaggerating," I say. "He was a good doctor."

"No," he replies, with euphoric intensity. "He was a dwarf!"

"What does that have to do with anything?" I ask. "Now you're picking on people's physical disabilities. You, of all people, making these kinds of discriminations?"

He looks at me in confusion. Then he throws his arms up in the air with that deprecatory air he assumes from time to time.

"Come on," he exclaims. "He was normal!"

A Voyage to Crete

Why do they insist on bringing a portable elevator over to the airplane to lower him down to the ground? It's coming slowly toward us like a castle across the incandescent, blindingly bright runway until it hooks on to the forward door of the plane like a harpoon. I tried, in vain, to explain to the Greek pilot that just as Paolo had boarded the airplane by the stairs, so he could debark by them.

"Maybe in Italy," he had said, as if alluding to some exotic country (and maybe he was right), "but not in Greece!"

And so, Paolo, taking precedence over all the other passengers, is lowered slowly to the tarmac of Heraklion airport, on the island of Crete, like a gift from the heavens being lowered onto a stage by a piece of theatrical machinery. I can just imagine his embarrassment (which is really ours), as well as his pride. It's much better for him if they exaggerate his handicap than if they minimize it. When he comes out of the elevator cabin, aided by a stewardess who seems very taken with her role, he smiles into the sun, shielding his eyes with his hand and waving without actually seeing us.

The monumental Babylonian hotel (who ever went to Babel anyway?) sits on top of a small hill. Landscaped into its slopes, which extend all the way down to the sea, are terraces, restaurants, swimming pools, and dance floors. From where we're standing we can see a cluster of tiny bungalows on the distant beach.

"Ours is the last one, right next to the water." I point out to him proudly.

"You're crazy! I never should have let you decide," Franca exclaims.

"Why? What's the matter?" I ask.

"Him," she says, pointing at Paolo. "How will he ever make it all that way?"

"There's a *tapis roulant*," I say.

I read about it in the guidebook. I like the expression; *escalator* doesn't even begin to compare with it.

Franca leans out over the balcony. She scrutinizes the landscape until she can discern a group of tourists standing Indian file, rising motionlessly past the cypress trees, gliding over the grass in the golden light of sunset like beatific divinities ascending toward the restaurant in the unending light of the Aegean.

That night, on the white and circular restaurant balcony, from a corolla of lights situated high up in the dark, comes a voice from a loudspeaker extending a warm welcome, first in English and then in Italian, to Paolo. There's a smattering of applause, some of the diners look around the room, others turn to look right at us.

Franca blushes. I put down my glass, Paolo is pleasantly shocked.

"That's nice, don't you think?" Franca says.

"Yes," I say. "I just hope that they do it for all of them."

"All of whom?"

"All of the guests. I'm not sure they do it for all the other kids."

"Does it really matter?" Franca exclaims.

We compete by alternately attributing to each other our shared frustrations.

"It's nice of them," she adds. "That's all."

Paolo has trouble swallowing his food, letting us know he fears one of those discussions that he knows by heart.

"You're right," I say, reaching out and squeezing his hand.

"You're too self-conscious," Franca tells me after dinner. We're sitting together on a swing. Paolo is being accompanied to the balcony's edge by the waiter to look at the night sea—swollen, shining, and immense.

"Perhaps," I say. "But we'll see who's right."

There's always the temptation—irresistibly vulgar in its own way, but no less real—to think that any act of kindness will be tallied up and added to the cost of our stay, which already exceeds our budget but not our needs. I will eventually change my mind about this. At first, Paolo deters people. Then he attracts them. He has learned—out of natural talent and experience—that we look to others to have both our prosperities and our misfortunes forgiven. That's why he trusts in people. He knows it's the best way to kindle trust. He feels constantly something I experience only in moments of grace: affinity for the world. By the end of our week, he has become the Benjamin of that heterogeneous community, united by the most temporary of connections, proximity, and by the most pathetic of motivations, the obligation to have fun. He has become the most sought-after companion. It is as if his handicap were a kind of vacation within the greater vacation.

On other holidays, his handicap has incited hostility, not to mention aversion. It all depends on a series of factors—all of which are understandable though not always fair—such as the unpleasantness of his problems, the cost of the stay, the weather, the season, local traditions, majority opinion, the courtesy of single individuals, faith and ideology, and, finally, culture (though I wouldn't rely too much on that). Civility can do a lot, but it's not enough. In one situation a person might be accommodating but in another situation that same person might show aversion. People who coexist with a handicap know that. So do people who don't.

The grotto where Zeus was born, on Mount Ida, is a wide crevasse that splits the earth diagonally. Once you have descended into it, the aperture above looks like a luminous hole in the heavens, obstructed by overhead brambles and supervised by soaring hawks. Down at the bottom are a series of dark damp caves, marked by time and the remnants of offerings.

Paolo leans against the mossy rock and doesn't move. More than patience, traveling with me has taught him how to surrender.

"Don't move," I say. "I'll come and help you."

I delicately pry his fingers away from the stone and help him over a dark rivulet. A shiver runs through me as I think about how senseless I have been to bring him all the way down here, down slippery paths that we will only have to climb again later—I don't know how—toward freedom.

Franca had refused to come with us.

"Where was Amaltea, the goat?"

"Here," I say, pointing out a deep niche in the rocks. I had told him that the Cretans were good liars, so I lie too, in honor of the island. I had also told him that in addition to Zeus's birthplace, you could see his death place.

"Where's his tomb?"

"They never found it."

This time I just can't bring myself to lie.

On the way back to the hotel, traveling over the high plains that are punctuated with windmills, we suddenly come across an abandoned building. Its locks are rusty and it's falling into ruins. I'm struck, in the silent wind of late afternoon, by an old neon sign on its roof: HOTEL ZEUS.

"How do we get to Lato?" I ask at the hotel.

"I suggest you don't go by car," the concierge replies in Italian.

"So how do we get there?"

"There's a taxi driver who can take you. Otherwise you'll ruin your car."

"It's probably better if we don't go," Franca says.

The concierge looks at her, a glimmer of understanding in his eyes.

"Why not?" I ask.

"The lady is right," the concierge says, still looking at her. "There are only ruins out there. The road itself is a ruin."

We're on our way to Lato with the taxi driver, the car bumping up and down as if it's crossing a dry riverbed. There are sandy patches, stony parts, pebbled areas, and expanses of dust and dirt. Paolo is thrilled.

"What's so special about Lato?" Franca asks.

"Two acropoleis on the mountains."

There they are, high up in the blue and green. The driver stops the car in an open area halfway along the valley, blocked in by low stone walls.

"I'll wait for you here," he says with a half smile, both in pity and as a challenge. He points out a steep path that winds up the barren hillside.

I help Paolo over the stones and ruins. We advance slowly, hunched over and contorted under the blazing sun.

"Let's take the shortcut," I say, pointing out some steps carved into the wall.

Never trust shortcuts (and not just those in the mountains) if you're trying to conserve your energy. Our fatigue is multiplied; the steps gradually transform themselves into a rock slide. I help Paolo along with my right hand, until he simply cannot go any farther. He can't get down. He grasps the wall, his arms and legs spread-eagled against it. I let myself slide back down in a tumble of stones to the path where Franca is standing, shaking her clasped hands at us in an act of disapproval or prayer, I'm not sure which. Then I climb back up toward Paolo. What am I doing? Who am I, standing here in this baking heat, in this valley, at four o'clock in the afternoon, panting, clawing at the cracks in this archaic fort? Things never feel quite so absurd as in moments of extreme danger, perhaps because they summon us to our destiny.

Sweat streaming down my face, I manage to grab Paolo by the ankles.

"Let go of the wall!" I yell.

He doesn't trust me.

When I finally manage to get him down and pass him on to Franca, who reaches up for him, I think of the deposition from the cross. I don't know why. He is exhausted but pleased. "I'm going to tell Alfredo about this," he murmurs, from where he's lying on the ground.

"You'll see him in three days, when we get home," Franca says, also flat on the ground, her arms open to the sky.

Lucent Crete: sunset, leaves on the trees, terraced vineyards, the car crawling along between rocky walls. The high Minoan road, which traverses the mountains of the island, is now behind us. The sea is not far away, the sun is on the horizon. There's a sudden peace. Silence and ruins on the hillside.

"Stop," I say to Franca, who's driving.

But it has already passed.

We stop at a restaurant on the coast. The sun filters through the reeds covering the pergola. A giant Greek salad, colorful and refreshing. Franca ordered the spicy cheese, Paolo the grilled fish.

"Homeric food," I say.

It has less effect now than when I said it two days ago at the Hotel dei Cureti, facing Mount Ida, a large platter of roasted mutton on the table. Never repeat yourself. They no longer notice the cleverness; they notice that you're repeating yourself.

I look at the waves breaking on the beach below, between the rocks. A few suntanned kids glide along the crest of the waves.

"How about a swim?" I ask Paolo with a smile, avoiding Franca's eyes.

"Now that's enough," I hear her say.

I look at her. She doesn't know what to make of things anymore.

I do. I know she's generous and indomitable. She puts up with two great burdens. I don't know which of us is a heavier load, him or me. I place my hand gently on her shoulder. She can guess what I'm thinking. I smile; my eyes are shiny. I raise my glass of resinous white wine.

"To Franca," I say.

Paolo, amazed that I didn't say *mamma*, raises his glass too.

We go for our swim at night, under the stars, in front of our bungalow. The water is salty and warm. Paolo has finally learned how to do the breaststroke, taking deep breaths and dunking his head under the water. When he emerges from the glimmering surface, I tell him he looks like a dolphin. He keeps doing it until he's exhausted, like I would do when I was young, when I knew someone was watching me. He floats on his back, panting, facing the sky.

"Come back!" Franca calls to us from the shore.

In front of the Heraklion Museum, leaning against the wall in the bright luminous colors of the afternoon, is a row of horse-drawn carts.

Paolo points them out to me. "Don't you want me to ride in one?"

I look at him, crestfallen. "But you don't need one," I say. "Why do you want to go in one?"

"Because it's less tiring," he replies.

Put Yourself in His Shoes

Bertoia, an elderly man who's ill, comes to visit me occasionally. I'm not really sure what he's got; he's reticent about discussing it. When asked, he becomes elusive, raising his eyebrows in a threatening way. He's slightly cross-eyed. He follows conflicting therapies that have gradually deformed his body. He's extremely thin and fragile. I see something of Don Quixote in him—not Cervantes's but Doré's. He walks into my study like an engraving, a mass of lines preparing themselves for decomposition.

"Have you ever tried putting yourself in your son's shoes?" he says at a certain point.

Is this a question or an accusation? "Well, I try and imagine his reactions," I say.

"No," he says, shaking his finger at me.

It's an accusation.

"You have to do more than that," he says, staring off into space, the creases under his eyes deepening. "You have to get into his head!"

"But I can't," I say.

"What do you mean you can't?" he asks darkly, hunching

over as if to protect himself from an attacker. But he's the one attacking here. "I did!"

I lean back dismally in my chair. Why has he come to see me? Why now? It's late July, my most coveted moment: vacation in the city after exams. I've been planning for months to read *Five Weeks in a Balloon* by Verne. Who gives him the right? He always felt like my protector. Formerly an accountant at the Art Institute, he was a zealous bookkeeper, a devotee of schedules, a maniac in an almost mystical phase of life.

"I often think about your son," he says. "I have gotten into his head."

He looks like he's hallucinating. I'm not sure if it's the illness or the medicines that make him feverish.

"You should too," he adds. "You'll see how well you'll understand him."

I understand it's a monstrous proposition but I try anyway. Who else will listen to us if not the insane?

I try to think, *I am Paolo*, but am struck by a sense of terror and vertigo. I have neither his past nor his future, I cannot imagine what he imagines, I cannot share in anything he experiences. We can never, as they say in that ruthless and horrid expression, get into someone's brain.

"I can't put myself in his shoes," I say.

He extends his skinny arms along the length of the chair and proudly raises his hollow face. "What about an actor?"

"They do it for fun," I say. "They're neither themselves nor the other."

"Can I tell you what I think?" he asks, looking straight ahead of him.

"Of course." People only ask that when they think badly of you.

"You are trapped in your own egoism."

"That may well be," I say firmly.

He has that horrible air about him that older people have when all they can do is predict the misfortune to come. Maybe Cassandra didn't have a choice, she simply foretold the future.

"Step outside yourself," he says, "and get into Paolo's head."

"No, I'll stay in mine," I reply. "He'd prefer it that way too, believe me."

He grips the arms of the chair, like a monarch at the theater. "Then you will never know," he says, raising his bony finger, "exactly who your son is."

That's right, I think to myself, I won't.

Scolding

I lent him an expensive camera for a school trip and he forgot it on the train. He takes rather interesting photographs. It's not so much the fleeting moment that he captures as the precarious point when his eye blinks and his body precipitates forward. His pictures, at times oblique and with slanted shafts of light, communicate a mobile and adventurous existence, the complete opposite of the posed universe that haunted the official class photographers in the schools of my youth.

I give him a scolding, condensed to its essence. Rapidly. I believe that rapidity, in scolding, is a much appreciated quality. The unpopularity of sermons, in any given situation, derives more from their preconceptions than from any particular accusations. My parents, in the recent Paleolithic age, held the superstitious belief that litanies of words produced great works. "Never tell lies! Do you understand? Under no circumstance!" fathers used to say, dazed by the very lies they were telling. Then, only a few minutes later, when the phone would ring, they'd shout out, "I'm not home for anybody! Do you hear?"

Then came the age when conventional psychoanalysis transformed our children into toys whose movements could be programmed. "He demolished the motorbike and now he expects me to punish him," said a young colleague of mine, for whom paternity seemed like a marvelous opportunity to try out pedagogical theories. "So without punishing him," he went on to say, "I bought him another one. I surprise him, you see? I disorient him. That's how I teach him."

His son was effectively disoriented. I didn't follow all the phases of his education but I do know he was the first one in his age group to try drugs. But I don't want to establish a relationship of cause and effect here. It's certain that the son, taking everything into account after the accident, couldn't have been too comforted. His weak father didn't even consider him worth scolding.

Paolo listens to me. I have a serious discussion with him. He's starving for seriousness; he never has fun when I'm having fun with him. I know it, but I continue to have fun with him by returning to that phrase he uses when a joke bombs, that idiotic alibi "But it was a joke!"

This time I say, "You made a mistake. You won't be able to use the camera for a few months."

He replies, "Thank you for talking to me about it man to man."

I tell my colleague.

"Disabled children are more mature," he says.

The Electroencephalogram

Another word that always threw me into a panic is electroencephalogram. I associated it, mistakenly, with alterations of the brain, deformations of the mind, a loss of thought processes. A reading would have shown us what was wrong inside his head. And I was shocked by the general indifference surrounding a word that meant, for me, a crack in his liberty (when we talk about liberty we all become legal scholars, wrangling over intangible definitions).

If I think how my fears have changed over the years, I could synthesize them this way: by accepting the cracks. It makes me think of the recurrent imprecation in the adventure novels by Salgari—"You old wreck!"—used indiscriminately for people or sinking ships. It's something of a piratical antidote to the cult of the body, which in its obsession with healthy diets and hormonal regimes seeks to fix the ongoing metamorphosis of the human organism in the immutable perfection of a butterfly.

That the thought of being handicapped is disconcerting to young people is, in itself, a tribute to growing up. Eternity lasts until the age of forty, ambitions are soberly reduced to a single word: everything. Then, as the years advance, some people regress toward a kind of retrospective youth. The most euphoric among them only try, but the stupid ones actually succeed. But the handicap, in the meantime, has become an appendage, a familiar experience; it becomes real and visible in others before finally rooting itself in us. The small omissions that we forgive ourselves become the unforgivable dormant craters of our elders' memory, of our future. To challenge one's limits as an end to itself (otherwise known as the fashionable imperative) derives from the fear of accepting one's limits. Never before as in this age has pushing beyond one's limits constituted an escape from recognizing them.

When I think about the questions I used to ask myself about Paolo's intelligence, I wonder about the ones I should have been asking about my own. And when I look around for inspiration, I don't find many comforting examples. We tend to isolate the occasional brilliant comments that we hear; they become memorable and help us scan the phases of our lives. The idiotic ones cancel each other out; they do nothing to better the quality of our lives. While encephalograms might show no damage, they will always be less telling than other tests. Handicaps, whether mental or physical, are far more subtle than they appear to be; we are closer to our limitations than to overcoming them.

I finally stopped being scared by the encephalogram and by IQ tests. (Why not test for stupidity as a planetary epidemic?) I think we should measure all things less; there are too many risks for everyone involved. I would propose a greater sense of delicacy with the handicapped and more respect. They will return the favor.

Garbage

He spoke at a student rally. I found out about it from a colleague of mine who has a friend who teaches at Paolo's school.

"How did it go?" I asked, trying to appear calm.

"Very well," she said, also seeming calm. "He was very clear."

"Do you know what he said?"

"I don't know the details," she said, "but the point was: Either we get treated like mature people or we'll force them to treat us like children."

I recognize the binary structure of his logic.

"I hear that you spoke at a rally," I say at home that evening.

"Yes, that's right," he says.

"How did it go?"

"It went well."

That's his laconic and exhaustive formula for replies.

"Did you have trouble with your voice?"

"There was a microphone."

"With all the difficulty you have speaking," I say, looking at him straight in the eye to overcome my trepidation, "weren't you scared?"

He looks at me. He seems glad I asked.

"You know, I thought about it," he says slowly, in that complicit and expert way of his, "and I realized that there were two possibilities. Either they were going to treat me like garbage or let me talk."

"And?"

"They let me talk."

The Recital

It's the end-of-the-year recital for the disabled children at Paolo's church youth group.

"Do you think I can go?" I ask Franca in desperate nonchalance.

"Of course," she says openly.

"What?" I ask her in disbelief.

"It's the third year he's done it, and you've never been once." She's trying to be neutral. "I suppose you could continue not going."

"How did he feel about me not being there?"

"Terrible."

"Did he say so?"

"No, you know how proud he is. He only asked if you were coming this year."

"What did you say?" Why do I even ask? Never ask questions.

"I don't know. I said, 'You know how Papa is.' "

"How is Papa?" I ask her.

"Terrible," she says, as if she were talking to Paolo.

I'm giving in. "What play are they doing?"

"*Ulysses.*"

"Whose, Joyce's?"

"No, Homer's."

I gave in.

Here I am in the auditorium, unadorned except for the metal folding chairs that surround the stage. An intense light shines from behind the heavy black curtain that hangs on rings along a metal bar. Portable spotlights project intersecting colored lights onto the whitewashed ceiling.

"This place looks like a bomb shelter," I say to Franca, who doesn't share the memory, because of her age, or the joke, because of her beliefs. She looks at the roomful of bright faces. There's a festive air. We're part of a warm, welcoming crowd that breaks into applause now and then to encourage the actors in benevolent complicity. In fact, the show has already begun. We are living it in the orchestra, in this gathering of desperate, resigned, happy, serious parents. A boy with Down's syndrome sticks his head out of the curtain, looks around the room, laughs, and retreats. Then a girl steps out but she runs off too. We hear clattering and shouting as they take their positions. Suddenly, recitals of my own infancy come flashing back; it wasn't about speaking memorable lines onstage; it was about the orchestra, darkness punctuated with eyes and lights. For us, theater was the audience for whom we made faces that we thought were hysterical. The theater was never again like that. The line that divided the actors from the audience seemed open to us in both directions. Yet it could not be crossed. We were bewitched by its magic.

I try to hold back my emotions.

"Do you like it?" Franca asks.

"Yes, enormously."

Here I open a parenthesis that has evil as its object.

We're used to evil. Evil has the power of confirming our superiority or relieving our weakness. It's so familiar that it makes good seem disconcerting, so we try to reduce it, mutating its signs and assimilating it into the negative models that are already familiar to us.

I've noticed this happening in the most common of reactions, including my own, toward voluntarism. The tendency is to interpret altruism as a stand-in for egoism, generosity as gratifying for the one who exercises it, solidarity in the name of self-interest, a sacrificing *I* being blackmailed by a tyrannical super-*I*. Nor can anything be learned from ethology, which has been ransacked in order to explain aggressiveness but never the other way around. Animals that sacrifice themselves for their young or for others—are they, too, victims of a super-*I*? No, that's instinct, ethologists tell us. But we continue to deny this positive instinct in man and instead endow him with all sorts of others.

Evil—contrary to what is generally thought—is reassuring. We venerate it in monsters; it justifies vendettas; it mobilizes our defenses and hardens the heart. Good is inimitable. (How can it ever be compared to evil?) It leaps over the trenches and walls we construct against the enemy, it eludes the endless little tricks of intelligence, it derails shrewdness by flat-out ignoring it, it's disarmed, and it's simple. Evil excites us and piques our curiosity, it stimulates the investigative spirit, it's hidden in the final room, the one where the infamous secret lies. Good opens doors; it doesn't hide anything; it steps aside so as not to be noticed. Evil promises mystery; good is a luminous mystery, an unacceptable presence.

I am speaking with full cognizance, but I am in good—if limited—company. For many men, nothing is more edifying than destruction and nothing is more repugnant than edification. That the ideologies of our century have been responsible for generating massacres is not because they pointed out some remote paradise but because they first had to create an immediate inferno. Of course, it's far more comforting—and more ethical—to turn the hierarchies on their heads. It's an alibi you can say anything about except that it hasn't been used.

Am I exaggerating? Maybe, but exaggerations, like caricatures, can offer us an image in which we can discern the original.

I had always imagined voluntarism—without knowing it, of course—as a point of intersection between a failed vocation and self-consolation. Until I met Paolo's friends. The kids that go out with him for pizza or to the movies or to the used record stores, where he'll buy popular songs from previous eras (who else to save our traditions if not the young?) are kind, gentle, and discreet. They don't expect anything in exchange, no gifts or thank-you notes. Not only do they help, they do what people need even when they never get it: They sympathize.

Paolo is spending the vacation with us but he doesn't consider it a vacation. I still don't know exactly what he considers it, nor do I intend to inquire. I wonder what we are communicating to him when, after fifteen years of injunctions, we still say, "Walk straight!" Is it an order, a reminder, an exhortation? An alibi for us to continue hoping? Is it disillusion, a scolding, a form of punishment? I've often noticed something other than exasperation in his look—an atrocious boredom masked by patience. If he finally manages to have fun on vacation with his group of volunteers, where they accept him with brio, without wanting to change him, should we even wonder why? The hidden imperative of the educator, according to Droysen, can be reduced to these few unsaid words: "You must become the way I want you, because only in that way will I ever be able to have a relationship with you." Is it any surprise that Paolo is happy when he is no longer being educated?

In classical times, pagans were disturbed to see fellow citizens help the poor, the sick, and the imprisoned. Today, when even laypeople practice charity (what does *lay* actually mean when the predominant religion is the religion of man?), people tend to profit from voluntarism rather than use it as a model.

By pretending not to see evil, we are reflected back in it. This is less true of goodness. For an author, however, evil is a saving grace and good is a curse. The praise of good troubled the great writers; it was the nightmare of their consciousness. In order to be excused for it, Manzoni took refuge in irony; Cervantes in madness; Dickens in stupidity; Dostoyevsky in idiocy; Melville in innocence. The only writer who never hesitated to raise a cathedral to good is Victor Hugo, but we can forgive him for anything.

To speak well of good is unforgivable. In fact, I can't forgive myself. But I simply had to pay back the friends, relatives, and strangers for the inestimable help they've given.

. . .

Suddenly, the curtain opens. A boy pushes it back. It slides along the rod. He keeps pushing it back until he bumps into the pole that holds it up. Laughter—practically an ovation—rises from the audience of disabled children and their families. I don't know whether the director—his name was on the poster— had meant for it to happen. It certainly couldn't have started any better. And it only got worse.

To say that everything possible happened would only be a part of it. There was a gigantic Ulysses with hairy legs and a white skirt who looked like a Scot who had descended on Asia Minor in sandals. Calypso's tears flowed as she sat on her egg of an island, wooden waves sliding by as if in a cartoon. Telemachus was the only person onstage who wasn't disabled, but you wouldn't have known it. He was a student of pharmaceutical science, Franca said. From his articulation and intonation we couldn't tell if he was asking Athena a question or answering her. They chose to take advantage of Paolo's cavernous voice to transform him into a laconic Polyphemus. I have to confess that his dialogue with Ulysses was very suggestive, a cross between the Levantine and the metaphysical, but maybe it was my emotions that betrayed me.

The best parts included the piece with Nausicaa, who sat by the edge of a river all dressed in white (the Down's syndrome daughter of a lawyer with wild eyes seated in the front row), and the banquet of Proci, with the companions gorging themselves on glasses of orange soda and prosciutto sandwiches. I have never liked seeing actors eat onstage, both because I couldn't join in and because they never really ate, just chomped away on microscopically small portions of food with hermetically sealed mouths. They never finished their food, they were always well-mannered, and they always sat up straight. That acting technique went unheeded in this play. Instead, I found myself envying the actors' everyday voracity. And they enjoyed displaying it to us, laughing along with the public as they gulped down slices of cake or devoured pieces of chocolate. Only Penelope, dressed in her brown tunic (a symbol perhaps of her conjugal faithfulness), managed to conserve a distant austerity worthy of Ionesco.

A well-earned, enthusiastic, and appreciative ovation rewarded everyone at the end of the show, actors and audience alike. Unanimity, that daydream of children and infinite utopia of those who never grow up, became a melancholy Eden.

We wait for Paolo to come out from behind the curtain. Finally he appears, triumphant, at the top of the stairs. He descends the first few steps, sweaty and glowing, refusing any help with a wave of his hand. Then he slips on the last two steps, pitching forward. Luckily we are at the bottom, where parents like to be and their children don't. He is saved by a final round of applause from the public, this time celebrating reality.

The Banquet

My father-in-law is eighty years old. He has taken good care of his body for his whole life, but now he's growing disabled in the mind. "No, it's not Alzheimer's," the famous gerontologist told us when we took him to get his opinion, pretending it was just a regular checkup. "Nor is it senile dementia," he said.

"So what is it then?" Franca asked.

The gerontologist looked at her with a careful smile. "It's old age, Signora."

When the best gerontologists get old, they tend to let down their guard and use basic language instead of shielding themselves behind professional jargon. Eventually they profess not to be of any help at all. But Franca refused to give in.

"Fine, but why did it get worse all of a sudden?"

"Because it's in the descendant phase of the parabola," the gerontologist replied, tracing an arc with his finger over the desk and holding up a copy of *National Geographic* to intersect it at its lowest part.

"Yes, but why his brain?" Franca insisted. "*His* mother," she said, pointing at me, "was completely lucid when she died, and she was older than my father."

"It's all written in our genes, Signora," the clinician said solemnly. "Your father's brain is aging at a faster rate than the other parts of his body. There's nothing strange about it."

Franca listened to him in dismay, almost in fear.

"You've done X rays and CAT scans," she said. "What did you see? What's happening to his brain?"

"Now don't get upset, Signora," the doctor replied. "This is a very common process. I'd have to say that his case doesn't even classify as precocious."

"What did you see?" Franca asked again.

"Atrophy in the cerebral cortex, with a deepening of the furrows and a dilation of the ventricles," the clinician replied, finally taking refuge in a cold, professional manner.

He held up his hand in a fist.

"Imagine a sponge. Some areas become spongelike. Connections are interrupted, some parts get lost."

"How horrible!" Franca murmured.

"No, Signora, don't think of it like that," the geriatrician said. "There are worse illnesses, which impair the brain and have devastating consequences."

Franca looked at him, undone.

"It's useless to deceive oneself: these symptoms don't go away. We may, however, be able to slow down the process of disintegration. He might require care but not full-time help. Your father ought to be able to lead a seminormal life."

"Until when?" Franca exclaimed, flushing with distress. "He's already not himself!"

"Unfortunately, that's one of the eventualities of his condition," the geriatrician said, in a serious voice. "Often, when our parents age they become what we, as children, were for them: vulnerable, needy. You are becoming the mother of your father. You have to be up to it."

He glanced at her to see the effect of his words and immediately looked down again. Franca, for whom her father had always been a reference point, wasn't ready to become one herself.

"Allow me to give you some advice, as well as a prescription." The doctor gestured vaguely toward a pad resting in a crystal dish. "Try and contradict him as little as possible."

"All right," Franca said.

"And don't tell him he contradicts himself; that will only augment his state of panic. Comply, let him be right. It's the lesser of two evils."

"What if he gets angry because he thinks I haven't been to see him when actually I've been there only two hours before?"

"Ignore it. Learn to lose your memory too," the doctor had said. "You'll see how good it'll make you feel. Oblivion is a powerful tool."

Then he turned toward me.

"Without the power of forgetting we wouldn't be able to survive," he said. "Give him room, trust me."

"What about names?" Franca had asked. "What about when he gets stuck on names?"

"Names—of course." The doctor opened his arms wide as if he were greeting an old friend. "Let him struggle with them. Doesn't it ever happen to you?"

"What?"

"To forget people's names."

"Why, sure."

"And yet, you're young. We call it benign forgetfulness; it

starts at about forty. The phenomenon is a little bit different in his case. Eventually he will begin to forget names for ordinary things."

There was a brief pause.

"It's common," he said. He liked that adjective; it gave him distinct pleasure. "We call it anomia."

"For him it's a tragedy," Franca had said.

The tragedy began—and it's not a rare evolution—as comedy. We all forget names, but the first sign of aging is not to forget them but to struggle to remember. Another sign is involving everyone around you in that incessant search, creating debts as well as hidden comparisons. "Now, what's his name?" has statistically proven to be the most frequent question aging people ask. It's also the least interesting, because it caters to their needs alone. My father-in-law began to be inexorably drawn to these kinds of questions, until ultimately he came to seem what he feared most: someone who's lost his memory.

A small didactic parenthesis: Anyone with minimum teaching experience knows that a student under examination hears questions no one has asked. He or she will search vainly for answers to these questions and in so doing embarrass the teacher who had originally wanted to help. If asked to comment on a poem, for example, the student is not expected to know the date and place it was written or the person to whom it might have been dedicated. But knowing that information is missing, the student is compelled to confess.

I've always advised my students not to reply sincerely to indiscreet questions about their knowledge of a subject. (This is

Italy, after all!) I've urged them not to admit their ignorance but to defer that information somehow. Only the worst students ever actually listened to me, learning to delay the invasive curiosity of their examiners by procrastination. The best students could never stand up to the challenge; they'd irrevocably confess their lacunae and surrender themselves instead to the ordeal of faithfulness, guilt, and punishment. It's a fascinating point of convergence. It demonstrates how sacrificial will in antiquity didn't concern the priests and their faithful alone but their victims too. It's a solid circuit that reinvents itself continuously.

My father-in-law began with simple mnemonic forays, which were as bothersome as they were unjustifiable. He insisted in particular on names, dates, places, and titles, which his interlocutors generally ignored. The unevenness of this game produced a losing winner; his opponent's ignorance could never compensate for his own amnesia. Gradually, though, the roles were reversed.

My mother-in-law, for example, took an unanticipated revenge on the man who for fifty years had imposed an authoritarian yoke on her (*coniugium:* "both people under the same yoke" is a word coined by the Romans, a people who knew about yokes, conjugality, and authority). Suddenly, the man who had heedlessly grilled everyone, the man who had laughed at her when she couldn't remember Tasso's first name (Torquato! he had shouted at her so that she could finally include the name in her crossword puzzle) could no longer remember the word for grape. "You know, those small red things we eat in autumn," he would start to grumble. "Berries," my mother-in-law would say. "No, not berries," he would reply impatiently. (No one is as impatient as the person who gets impatient with someone who can't help them remember.) "Blackberries," my mother-in-law would say, beginning to enjoy herself. "What?" my father-in-law would complain. "You don't eat blackberries in the fall." "Of course you do," my mother-in-law would reply, now seriously offended. "Both in the summer and in the fall." "Well, not blackberries," my father-in-law would say in desperation. Then he would try to clarify things. "You squash them to make a drink." "Oranges," my mother-in-law would exclaim, throwing out a wrong word so that he'd be even farther from the right one. I'm certain that she'd deny it just as much as she desired it, at least unconsciously (let's not deny her the alibi that we've extended to everyone else). My father-in-law would give up in humiliation, staring into space, probably trying to find the word on his own. Sometimes his face would light up and he would joyfully shout out the name.

"Grapes! Grapes!" he'd say in exultation, over and over, and then he'd get angry with her. "Why didn't you think of it? I told you they were small and red."

"What are?" my mother-in-law would ask, knowing the game would begin all over again. My father-in-law would retreat, struck by a new sense of anguish.

"Go get the dictionary," he'd say, gleaning from the imperative the grammatical mode of his life. My mother-in-law would look up the word *grape* and read him the entry like a bureaucrat until she got to the word *bunch*.

"That's it," my father-in-law would say excitedly. "Bunch! A bunch of grapes!"

The last time he came to dinner I noticed how much his condition had worsened. He couldn't remember my name at all. When he talked to Franca he would simply point at me and say "him." It might have been the pronoun that he always used to talk about me in private, but in public it made me feel uncomfortable.

We also invited Marco over to dinner. "Hello, where's Antonio?" my father-in-law said to him when he saw him in the entrance. "I don't know, who's Antonio?" Marco replied. "He's my son," my father-in-law said impatiently. "No, I'm your son," Marco said.

My father-in-law, vexed, walked up to him and looked him straight in the eyes. "I know," he said. Then, after a pause, he added, "So you're Antonio." "No, I'm Marco," the other had replied.

It's his circulation, the doctor explained. Alterations in blood pressure, metabolic variations. In fact, when my father-in-law sat down in the living room across from Marco, he began to regard him as his son. Marco started telling his father about his veterinary practice.

Because Marco had a tracheotomy to remove a tumor, every time he wants to speak he has to press a valve under his shirt at about the height of his sternum. If he doesn't press it at the right time his voice comes out at first aphonally, like in a horror film, and then bubbly, and finally, when the hole closes over again, raucously but clear. He went through the operation and a course of postoperative treatment without complaining, at least to other people, which many would agree is an admirable quality. "Heroic" had been my own definition, an adjective that at the time gathered popular consent.

Marco, sitting in an armchair facing my father-in-law, puts his hand under his shirt and, after a scratchy sound, like an old crystal set, says that his practice is growing, despite the operation.

"What operation?" my father-in-law asks.

Marco points to his throat and, in a voice that explodes from inside, replies impassively, "This one."

My father-in-law doesn't say anything. He knows Marco isn't fooling him, but he just can't remember. He looks at me to see if I can help but he never expected much from me, still less on an occasion like this.

He exerts himself fiercely to smother his dismay.

"Shall we go to table?" he asks.

I don't think I'll invite them over again. Family reunions have a lugubrious quality. Given the physical or mental difficulties of any of the members, it's better not to make things worse by putting additional pressure on them, even if some mental handicaps can be a source of humor. Drunks and amnesiacs know a thing or two about that, though I never really understood why, perhaps because the world finally appears upside down. Still, it's good not to let down one's guard.

I'm afraid that's precisely what happened the other evening. I too suffer from a problem that occasionally disturbs me. I lose my voice. It's a form of aphony. Ambushed by my emotions and undone by the retreat of this or that capacity—not unfamiliar to the respiratory tract and mouth or to the labors of teaching— my voice folds in on itself, gets lower, turns into a ghost, disappears, and then comes back, altered. "Your unconscious doesn't want you to teach anymore," a specialist once told me. "Unfortunately, the problem is my consciousness," I replied.

The other evening I rationed out my interventions, distributing my voice in calibrated doses. "Normal people can speak with no limits," the specialist had said, "but not you. Your voice is a tank, it has a limit, like a car, and you shouldn't go into reserve or you'll break down. For how long? Maybe only for a little while, as long as it takes to replenish itself. But it's better to stop earlier and avoid inconvenience."

To avoid inconvenience I let other people talk, which actually is the most appreciated form of behavior in someone who invites you over to listen to what you have to say. At a family gathering, however, abstention is judged with suspicion. When I spoke, my voice came out sounding crackly and dry, like an otherworldly whisper.

My brother-in-law pressed the valve under his shirt.

"What did you say?"

I swallowed to gain time and to breathe. Paolo, who understands my disability because of his own, answered for me in his raucous voice.

"He said that's not the point."

"Well, what is, then?" my father-in-law asked, with unexpected rapidity.

The entire evening he drove us crazy with his frenetic search for the most common words: bicycle, taxes, beer, school, summer. He thought up the most labyrinthine paraphrases for a word as simple as fish. The things that live underneath. Worms? No. Miners? No. Speleologists? How ridiculous! That live under where? The stuff you drink. Water? Yes. Fish? Yes, fish! Fish! Was that so very hard?

Language had become a mined and dangerous field where any advance could prove fatal. We'd hesitate every step of the way. "What do you call . . . ?" was the exasperating beginning. And together we'd scout it out—worn out, het up, confused, oscillating between comedy and tragedy on the pendulum of life. When he ventured off into more abstract concepts like *virtue*, the need to define became more desperate than that of a convocation of philosophers. Sometimes, though, unlike them, we would have to end in an enlightened and superior state of defeat.

If he asked for a simple clarification, everything seemed normal. I decided to hold off explaining what the point was anyway. I waved it away with my hand, as if it were a minor case of indigestion. I put off solving this problem and others to the future.

Paolo, who knew that saying the most terrible things would make me laugh, asked, at midnight, when all our guests had left and only he and I were awake, "Will you become like that too?"

"I don't know." I laughed.

It was a hypothesis I had never thought of, though evidently it wasn't as improbable as it had once seemed.

And then, with the gloomy bravura that compensates for so much else in both him and in me, he added, "The problem is, what's going to happen to me?"

From a Distance

Occasionally, from a distance, I'll see him coming down the long narrow street where I live. He keeps close to the walls of the houses so there's something to lean on if he trips. He walks awkwardly. Instead of following his body's commands, his body weight seems to take advantage of him, lurching him forward suddenly.

Some people recognize him and say hello. He'll stop and lean against the wall, always glad to chat. I can tell that some people treat him like a child, the same people who treat children like idiots and who ultimately put themselves on an equal footing. He is capable of saying things that these people wouldn't even begin to understand, but he limits himself to smiling back at them.

People who see him for the first time are not always satisfied with one glimpse. They have to stop and turn around and look at him closer. He knows it when they do; I think he walks off with a pained expression. But maybe not, maybe he's just being careful. He's used to being watched. It's me who's relentless. It's my face with the pained expression. That's what unites us, from a distance.

Sometimes I shut my eyes and then quickly open them again. Who's that boy walking unsteadily near the wall? I've never seen him before. He's disabled. I try to think about what my life would have been like without him in it, but I can't. We can think of many lives, but we can never disavow our own.

Once, when I was watching him as if he were someone else and I were someone else, he waved at me. He leaned up against the wall and smiled. For a moment it was as if we were meeting for the very first time.

Born in Como in 1934, novelist and essayist Giuseppe Pontiggia was editor of *Verri* and co-editor of *L'Almanacco dello Specchio*. He is the best-selling and award-winning author of ten novels and a collection of essays. *Born Twice* was awarded a Strega Prize, Italy's most prestigious literary award, in 2001, and is his first major work to appear in English.

Oonagh Stransky was born in Paris in 1967. Awarded the American Literary Translators Association Fellowship in 2000, she has translated both prose and poetry. Currently she is working on the translation of a novel by Erminia Dell'Oro.

A NOTE ON THE TYPE

This book The text of this book was set in Electra, a typeface designed by W. A. Dwiggins (1880–1956). This face cannot be classified as either modern or old style. It is not based on any historical model, nor does it echo any particular period or style. It avoids the extreme contrasts between thick and thin elements that mark most modern faces, and it attempts to give a feeling of fluidity, power, and speed.

Composed by Creative Graphics,
Allentown, Pennsylvania
Printed and bound by R. R. Donnelley & Sons,
Harrisonburg, Virginia
Designed by Virginia Tan